FROM THE
NANCY DREW FILES

THE CASE: *On the day of her high school graduation Rachel Kline disappears.*

CONTACT: *Ned's friend Josh Kline fears his younger sister has been the victim of foul play.*

SUSPECTS: *Dennis Harper—he's hot, he's cool, and he doesn't play by the rules. When Rachel went out with him, she was flirting with danger.*

Mike Rasmussen—Rachel dumped him for Dennis, and he's still angry.

Jessica Bates—Rachel's classmate hangs all over Mike, and she seems to bear a special grudge against Rachel.

COMPLICATIONS: *Some of Beverly Hills's wealthiest homes have been burglarized, and many people —including the police—think that Rachel is involved.*

Books in The Nancy Drew Files™ Series

#1	SECRETS CAN KILL	#27	MOST LIKELY TO DIE
#2	DEADLY INTENT	#28	THE BLACK WIDOW
#3	MURDER ON ICE	#29	PURE POISON
#4	SMILE AND SAY MURDER	#30	DEATH BY DESIGN
#5	HIT AND RUN HOLIDAY	#31	TROUBLE IN TAHITI
#6	WHITE WATER TERROR	#32	HIGH MARKS FOR MALICE
#7	DEADLY DOUBLES	#33	DANGER IN DISGUISE
#8	TWO POINTS TO MURDER	#34	VANISHING ACT
#9	FALSE MOVES	#35	BAD MEDICINE
#10	BURIED SECRETS	#36	OVER THE EDGE
#11	HEART OF DANGER	#37	LAST DANCE
#12	FATAL RANSOM	#38	THE FINAL SCENE
#13	WINGS OF FEAR	#39	THE SUSPECT NEXT DOOR
#14	THIS SIDE OF EVIL	#40	SHADOW OF A DOUBT
#15	TRIAL BY FIRE	#41	SOMETHING TO HIDE
#16	NEVER SAY DIE	#42	THE WRONG CHEMISTRY
#17	STAY TUNED FOR DANGER	#43	FALSE IMPRESSIONS
#18	CIRCLE OF EVIL	#44	SCENT OF DANGER
#19	SISTERS IN CRIME	#45	OUT OF BOUNDS
#20	VERY DEADLY YOURS	#46	WIN, PLACE OR DIE
#21	RECIPE FOR MURDER	#47	FLIRTING WITH DANGER
#22	FATAL ATTRACTION	#48	A DATE WITH DECEPTION
#23	SINISTER PARADISE	#49	PORTRAIT IN CRIME
#24	TILL DEATH DO US PART	#50	DEEP SECRETS
#25	RICH AND DANGEROUS	#51	A MODEL CRIME
#26	PLAYING WITH FIRE	#52	DANGER FOR HIRE

Available from ARCHWAY Paperbacks

THE NANCY DREW FILES CASE · 47

FLIRTING WITH DANGER

Carolyn Keene

AN ARCHWAY PAPERBACK
Published by POCKET BOOKS

New York   London   Toronto   Sydney   Tokyo   Singapore

This book is a work of fiction. Names, characters, places and incidents are either the product of the author's imagination or are used fictitiously. Any resemblance to actual events or locales or persons, living or dead, is entirely coincidental.

AN ARCHWAY PAPERBACK *Original*

An Archway Paperback published by
POCKET BOOKS, a division of Simon & Schuster Inc.
1230 Avenue of the Americas, New York, NY 10020

Copyright © 1990 by Simon & Schuster Inc.
Cover art copyright © 1990 Jim Mathewuse
Produced by Mega-Books of New York, Inc.

ISBN: 0-671-67499-4

First Archway Paperback printing May 1990

10 9 8 7 6 5 4 3 2

Printed in the U.S.A.

IL 7+

FLIRTING
WITH DANGER

Chapter

One

"THIS IS THE LIFE," Nancy Drew whispered to Ned Nickerson as he took a breakfast croissant from the tray held out by the uniformed maid.

Ned grinned and shrugged as he took a cheese danish from the same tray. "What can I say?" he whispered back. "I know how to pick my friends."

Nancy and Ned had arrived at the Beverly Hills home of Josh Kline, Ned's friend and college classmate, the night before. Josh, who was majoring in filmmaking at Emerson College, had landed a summer internship at a

1

famous Hollywood movie studio and had moved back home for the summer. He'd invited Nancy and Ned to visit, and they were both looking forward to an exciting vacation in Southern California.

"I can't believe you're ready to graduate from high school, Rachel," Karen Kline, Josh's mother, remarked from the end of the table. There was a rueful expression on her pretty, tan face. "It seems like yesterday that we brought you home from the hospital. Doesn't it, Allen?" she asked her husband, a lean, gray-haired man seated at her right.

Nancy looked on as Allen Kline beamed at his daughter. "We're really proud of you, Rachel."

Rachel Kline brushed a long lock of sun-streaked blond hair away from her face and gazed straight at her father. "I know," she said. "You've only mentioned it about fifteen times in the past week."

There was irritation in the girl's voice, Nancy thought. Karen Kline sighed, and Allen Kline reached out for his wife's hand. Nancy exchanged a look with Ned, who gave a slight shrug. There was a short silence as Rachel stared out through the French doors of the dining room at the aquamarine waters of the swimming pool with a distracted expression in her pretty brown eyes.

"I know I'm looking forward to going to your graduation," Nancy put in, trying to ease the tension.

"Me, too," Ned said. "After everything Josh has told me about Ocean Highlands High, I can't wait to see the place."

"It is pretty amazing," Josh said, glancing at his sister.

Rachel didn't meet his eye. Instead, she got up from the table. "If it's okay with you, I'm going to change."

Allen Kline cleared his throat and pushed back his chair. "That's fine, Rachel. I have to get going, too."

After Rachel and her parents had gone upstairs, Nancy and Ned lingered at the breakfast table, talking to Josh and making plans for the next few days.

"I can't wait to see the studio," Nancy told Josh excitedly.

"What else should we do?" Ned asked his friend.

"Let's see." Josh counted his fingers. "There's Malibu, and the tour of the stars' homes. Grauman's Chinese Theater. And you really should go up into the hills. You get a

3

great view of L.A. from there, especially at night. It's totally romantic."

Ned gave Nancy a wry grin. "Now, there's an idea," he said.

Nancy felt herself blushing but was secretly glad. Since Ned was away at school, they didn't get to spend too much time alone.

"We'll have to check it out," she said, giving him a light kiss on the cheek. "But right now, I think I have a couple of things to do."

She excused herself to go upstairs. After she left the spacious dining room for the entryway, Nancy glanced up at the huge crystal chandelier overhead. Like the rest of the house, it was spectacular.

Passing a mirror as she started up the elegant, curving staircase, Nancy smiled at her reflection. Her blue eyes were bright, and she'd pulled her shoulder-length, reddish blond hair back into a French braid. In a few days, she hoped, she would have a golden tan to take back to River Heights as a souvenir.

She just wished she could show this place to her best friends, Bess Marvin and George Fayne. It was as good as any of the sets on the TV soap operas.

Reaching the top of the stairs, Nancy turned left, heading toward her room. It was really more a suite than a room, with its own whirlpool bath and a view of the tennis court and swimming pool. Her sandaled feet sank into the thick blue carpeting.

She paused outside Rachel's room to say hello because the girl's door was open.

"Dennis, I can't do that!" came Rachel's voice, her tone hushed and serious. "You don't know how my parents are counting on this. I can't let them down!"

Just then Rachel turned and saw Nancy standing in the hallway, peering into her room. Her brown eyes widened with alarm, but in a flash she recovered and managed a shaky smile.

"Listen, I've got to go. I'll talk to you later," she said. Without another word she hung up the phone and turned to Nancy with a perfect smile. "One of my friends is a little nervous about the ceremony," she explained lightly. "He has to make a speech."

It occurred to Nancy that Rachel might be hiding something. She seemed too quick to explain away her conversation. Maybe it was nothing, but Nancy didn't think she had mistaken the troubled look in the girl's eyes.

Rachel went to her closet and took out a beautiful white dress with a pink satin sash. "I'll be wearing this to the graduation party," she said. "What do you think?"

5

"It's great," Nancy answered. Then she lifted one hand in a wave. "I'll let you go now. I'm sure you have a lot to do."

Rachel nodded. "I've got to go over to the school and pick up my cap and gown, for one thing," she said, sounding rushed and jittery. "And then there's my hair. . . ."

Nancy grinned. She could remember how nervous she'd been for her high school graduation. Maybe it was just edginess that was making Rachel act a little weird. She headed on to her own room, where she chose a turquoise sundress for the afternoon graduation ceremony. Then she flopped down on the bed to write postcards to her dad and George and Bess back home in River Heights. The girls would love to know what it was like to be a guest in a Beverly Hills mansion.

As she wrote Nancy kept pausing to think. She was sure she'd heard a note of desperation and fear in Rachel's voice while she was talking to her friend Dennis on the phone. Just what was it that Rachel couldn't do?

Several hours later the gym at Ocean Highlands High School was crowded with well-dressed, tanned people who all seemed to be talking at once. Nancy, standing beside Ned, craned her neck, trying to find Rachel among the eager seniors. The ceremony was going to begin in a few minutes, and there was no sign of her.

Ned took Nancy's arm and pulled her aside by the doors, which opened onto a breathtaking view of the Pacific Ocean. In the dazzling June sunshine, the sea looked as turquoise as Nancy's dress.

"Okay, Drew," he said, his eyes dancing with amusement, "what's bugging you?"

Nancy didn't even try to sidestep the question. Ned knew her too well for that. "I was looking for Rachel just now because I was worried about her. When I was passing her room this morning, I overheard her talking on the phone. She was really upset, Ned."

Ned frowned. "About what?"

"I don't know," Nancy said. "It was more her tone of voice than what she said. She sounded really scared."

"What did she say?"

"Something like, 'I can't do that—you don't know how much this means to my parents.'" Just then Nancy spotted Mr. and Mrs. Kline in the group of parents, guests, and graduates. They appeared to be anxious and a little worried as they approached Nancy and Ned.

"Have either of you seen Rachel?" Karen Kline asked them.

"No," Ned answered, trying to smile reassuringly. "She's got to be around here somewhere. After all, this is her big day."

"We'll help look, if you like," Nancy volunteered.

Mrs. Kline nodded gratefully. "That would be wonderful, Nancy," she responded. "Thank you."

"You go this way," Nancy told Ned, pointing to her right, "and I'll head over there. By the time we meet at the other end of the gym, we'll have found Rachel."

"Okay," Ned agreed, and he took off after the missing graduate.

Rachel was nowhere. Nancy even checked the girls' bathroom and backstage in the auditorium, where the ceremony would be held.

Nancy was really getting worried by the time she returned to the gym and found Ned. He hadn't had any better luck. Josh was with Ned, but he didn't share everyone else's concern.

"Don't worry about it, Nancy," Josh said. "Rachel likes being center stage too much to miss her own graduation. When her name is called, she'll be there to get her diploma."

Josh seemed pretty confident his sister would show up. "I hope you're right," Nancy said as Ned took her hand and led her into the auditorium after the Klines.

As soon as the crowd was seated the principal of Ocean Highlands High, Mr. Jeffries, greeted them. Then he introduced the valedictorian, who made the first speech. After several more speeches and award presentations, it was time for the graduates to get their diplomas.

The Klines and Ned and Nancy waited eagerly for Rachel's name to be announced.

"Rachel Kline!" Mr. Jeffries finally called out.

None of the students seated in front of the small stage stood up.

"Rachel Kline," the principal repeated, and still there was no response. There was a buzz in the audience, though.

Ned and Nancy exchanged a look. Josh bit his lower lip and glanced over at his father. Karen Kline sat up in her chair, her eyes desperately scanning the group of students in their caps and gowns.

"Rachel Kline!" the principal tried one last time, but the pretty blond girl didn't appear.

"Something terrible has happened, I just know it," Mrs. Kline whispered, her lips trembling. "Rachel's gone!"

Chapter

Two

ALLEN KLINE looked at his wife with a confused expression on his face. "There has to be a reasonable explanation, Karen," he whispered. "Maybe she got sick—"

"She probably thought she had time to go for a soda," Josh said, trying to comfort his mother.

"I'm sure she's okay," Nancy said. Inside, though, she wondered. Could this have something to do with the conversation she'd overheard earlier?

Around them, the graduation was continuing. "Come on," Nancy said to Ned. "Let's go out with the Klines."

Ned nodded, and they stood up to follow Allen Kline as he steered his wife out of the auditorium. Josh followed.

Outside in the hall, Karen Kline's face was pale beneath her carefully applied makeup. She reached out for her husband's hand. "I just know something terrible has happened— she'd *never* miss her own graduation!"

Ned spoke up. "Listen, Josh, I think your parents should go home and wait there to see if your sister calls. We can look for her."

"Great idea, Ned," Nancy said. "There's no point in your hanging around here," she told the Klines reassuringly.

Josh gripped his mother's trembling hands in an effort to calm her. "Ned and Nancy are right, Mom. You and Dad should go home. We'll try to find Rachel and catch a ride later."

Allen Kline wrapped his arm around his wife's shoulders. "Josh is right, honey. If Rachel is having a problem, she'll probably try to call us. We're not doing any good here." He turned to Josh, Nancy, and Ned. "We'll be waiting to hear from you," he said, and he led his wife out to the parking lot.

The applause from inside the auditorium

told Nancy the graduation ceremony was about to conclude. In another few minutes the hallway and gymnasium would be crowded with people, and that would make searching for Rachel even harder.

"Let's fan out and check inside the building again," she suggested. "If we don't find her, we'll search the grounds, too."

Ned glanced down at his watch. "Let's meet in the parking lot in half an hour and compare notes."

Nancy nodded thoughtfully. "I'd like to talk to some of Rachel's friends, find out when they last saw her. Do you know any of them?"

"There's Beth Hanford," Josh answered. "She's Rachel's best friend, so she'd know everybody they hang out with."

"Is there a special guy? I heard Rachel talking to someone this morning—I think his name was Dennis." If she could find Dennis, he might know where Rachel was.

Josh shrugged. "I don't think I've heard Rachel mention him, but Beth would know."

"Good—" Nancy began.

The wave of laughing graduates coming through the swinging doors of the auditorium interrupted Nancy. Soon parents and other well-wishers were crowded around them, taking pictures and offering hugs and congratulations.

"We'd better start looking for her," Ned said, nudging Josh.

"Right," his friend said. While the boys went in opposite directions to look for Rachel, Nancy approached one of the graduates and smiled.

"Excuse me," she said to the girl, who was adjusting the tassel on her cap, "but could you tell me where to find Beth Hanford?"

"Sure," the graduate replied, looking around. "That's her over there. The one with the dark hair and big hoop earrings."

Nancy spotted Beth standing between two happy people who were probably her parents. She made her way over through the milling, delighted crowd.

"Beth?" she said, smiling and holding out one hand. "My name is Nancy Drew, and I'm visiting with the Klines. I was wondering if you've seen Rachel today."

Beth's bright smile faded, and she shook Nancy's hand distractedly. "No," she answered slowly. "I thought it was weird that she didn't show up when they called her name."

"Did you speak to her at all today?" Nancy asked.

Beth's pretty face had virtually drained of color. "No. What's wrong? Has something happened?"

Mr. Hanford spoke up then. "Is there anything we can do to help?"

"I don't think so. Rachel seems to be missing, but her brother and my friend are looking for her."

"I hope she's okay," Mrs. Hanford said. "I'm sure her mom and dad are really worried."

Before Nancy could answer, Beth broke in. "I'd like to stay here and help look for Rachel," she said to her parents. "Would that be okay? I mean, is it all right if we celebrate later? I'd feel awful if I didn't try to find her."

Mrs. Hanford smiled gently. "Of course, dear. Your dad and I will be at home. Let us know if we can help."

"Thanks," Beth said to her parents. Then she turned to Nancy, pulling off her graduation cap. "The first thing I want to do is get out of this gown," she said. "It's really hot."

Nancy followed Beth into a room where special clothing racks had been set up and helped her out of the gown. Underneath it she was wearing a bright yellow dress with a high collar.

"Beth, do you think Rachel could have run away?" Nancy asked.

Beth appeared to be troubled for a moment. She started to say something, then stopped herself. Finally she murmured, "No. Rachel wouldn't run away."

"You're sure?" Nancy prodded. Was the girl covering for her friend? Beth seemed as if she might be holding something back.

She shook her head resolutely. "I'm sure. Running away is dumb, and Rachel knows that. Besides, things are good for her at home." She stared off for a moment, then met Nancy's eyes again. "I'm ready. Let's go."

Nancy led Beth back into the crowd of graduates milling around in the gymnasium by a table spread with sandwiches and sodas. "Does Rachel know anybody named Dennis?" she asked as the girls scanned the group for any sign of Rachel. "I heard her talking to him this morning, and she sounded pretty upset."

Beth's face paled visibly. "Dennis," she said to herself in a whisper. When she saw Nancy looking at her, though, Beth recovered quickly. "He's just a guy she hangs out with sometimes. No big deal."

"Did he go to school here at Ocean Highlands, too?" Nancy asked, being careful to keep her voice light. She didn't want Beth to get defensive. The girl seemed reluctant enough as it was.

"No," Beth answered as she and Nancy approached a group of kids. "I mean, yes, but he's older. He graduated last year."

"I see," Nancy replied, still trying to put Beth at ease. "Are he and Rachel serious about each other?"

Beth's eyes came quickly back to Nancy's face and widened. "You mean, are they in love?"

Nancy nodded, waiting.

Beth's expression was troubled. "They've been dating for a while, but I don't think they'd elope or anything like that. Rachel's parents would have a fit."

Nancy knew Beth was right. Even if she was in trouble, Rachel didn't seem like the type to just run off and worry her parents unnecessarily. If she had wanted to go off with Dennis, and her parents didn't approve of him, she might not have told them, though. Dennis seemed like the logical link to Rachel's disappearance.

"Did you see Dennis around this morning?" she asked.

Beth shook her head. There was still a scared expression in her eyes. Nancy found herself wondering again what the girl was hiding.

She was about to ask Beth another question when a good-looking guy with wavy brown hair and blue eyes came up to them. He was still dressed in his cap and gown.

"Have you seen Rachel?" he demanded angrily before Beth could say anything.

"No. I was hoping you had," Beth said. "Mike, this is Nancy Drew, a friend of the Klines. Nancy, Mike Rasmussen."

"Hi, Mike," Nancy said.

Nancy saw Mike's eyes take in her turquoise sundress. "Hi," he replied with new interest.

Beth was tapping her foot. "Never mind the flirting, okay, Mike? Nancy and I need to find Rachel. We're really worried about her, and her parents probably are, too. Haven't you seen her at all?"

Mike frowned. "She was here earlier. I saw her when I came to pick up my cap and gown."

"Was she alone?" Nancy asked.

"Yeah," Mike answered. His tone told Nancy he thought it was a stupid question.

"Did she seem to be worried about anything?" Nancy asked, choosing to ignore his attitude.

Mike thought for a moment. "Well, she was a little rushed. Now that I think about it, she didn't take her cap and gown at all. She just hung around for a few minutes, then left."

Nancy glanced at her watch. "I've got to meet Josh and Ned in the parking lot," she told Beth. "Maybe they've had better luck than we have."

"I hope so," Beth said, almost in a whisper. "I really hope so."

She and Nancy made their way through the diminishing crowd to the front doors of the high school. It was a big school, clean, well designed, and well built, and Nancy paused for a moment to admire the view of the ocean. She and Beth started toward the parking lot. There were still a lot of cars around, but she didn't spot Ned or Josh.

"Have you and Rachel been best friends for a long time?" Nancy asked.

"Since first grade," Beth confirmed. She stared down at the pavement for a few seconds. "She tells me everything—or I thought she did. You'd think she'd have mentioned it if she planned to skip graduation."

Nancy shaded her eyes from the bright afternoon sunshine and scanned the parking lot for Ned and Josh. Wherever they were, she hoped Rachel was with them, safe and sound. "Maybe something came up," she said. "Are you absolutely sure Rachel wasn't in any kind of trouble?"

Beth hesitated for a long time before answering. "Yes," she said finally. "I'm sure."

"Nancy!" a familiar masculine voice called. "Over here!"

Nancy spotted Ned calling to her. "Come on! I think we've found something," he shouted.

She and Beth sprinted toward the two boys, who were standing beside a silver Camaro in the far corner of the parking lot.

"It's Rachel's car," Ned explained when they caught up.

"There's no way she would have left her car behind," Josh stated. "It's practically like her baby."

Nancy didn't know what Josh had expected to find in the car. Was he hoping that Rachel would be sitting inside, waiting? Nancy knew Rachel's brother had been disappointed, though. It was empty.

Josh looked first at Ned, then at Nancy, his handsome face full of strain. "Are you thinking what I'm thinking?"

"What's that?" Nancy asked, studying his face.

"That my sister's been kidnapped!"

Chapter

Three

"KIDNAPPING ISN'T the only possibility, Josh," Nancy said gently, noticing that the keys were still in the ignition. She tried to catch Beth's eye. It appeared more and more likely that Rachel's friend was wrong about the girl not being in some kind of trouble. Rachel must have been in a big hurry if she'd left the keys in the car.

"Let's go back to your place and find out if your parents have heard anything," Ned said, laying a hand on his friend's shoulder. "Maybe Rachel's there, and we're all standing around worrying for nothing."

Josh checked out the silver Camaro again. "She's even left the keys in the ignition," he pointed out with a frown. "I don't like the look of this at all."

"Ned, why don't you and Josh take Rachel's car back to the house? Beth, can you drop me off?" The girl nodded. Nancy wanted another chance to try to find out what Beth wasn't telling her.

Josh nodded distractedly as he and Ned climbed into the Camaro. Beth led the way to a yellow Volkswagen.

Once they were in the car, Beth gave a little sigh and reached up to drape the tassel from her graduation cap over the rearview mirror. "This day isn't turning out at all like I thought it would," she said.

"No, I guess it isn't," Nancy said, feeling sorry for the girl. "Are you sure you've told me everything?" she ventured.

Beth swallowed hard. "I'm sure." Her expression told Nancy that she wasn't going to say anything more. Beth started the car.

"Everything will be okay" was all Nancy could say. She just hoped she was right.

When Nancy and Beth pulled into the Klines' driveway, Ned was waiting for them. Josh had probably gone inside to be with his parents.

"Is she here?" Beth asked eagerly.

Ned shook his head. "No. And the Klines were really upset when they found out Rachel had left her car."

Ned and Nancy and Beth found Josh watching his father talk on the telephone when they went inside. Mr. Kline was on the phone with the police, trying to file a missing persons report.

Nancy glanced at Ned. They both knew from experience that the police wouldn't be able to do a thing for twenty-four hours. Until that much time had passed, a person wasn't considered legally missing.

"I'm telling you, her car was found in the school parking lot!" Mr. Kline yelled into the receiver. "The keys were in the ignition! Now, that indicates that there is at least a possibility that our daughter has been kidnapped!"

"Where's your mother?" Nancy asked Josh in a quiet voice.

"Upstairs, in Rachel's room," Josh said. "She's pretty shook up."

Nancy excused herself and went upstairs with Beth close behind.

Karen Kline was sitting on Rachel's bed, crying softly. She looked up hopefully at the noise, but when she saw it was Nancy and Beth her face fell.

Beth sat down on the bed beside Karen Kline and said, "Please don't cry, Mrs. Kline. Rachel's probably going to come walking through the front door at any minute, with a perfectly good explanation."

"Has Rachel ever run away before?" Nancy asked, trying to keep her voice as gentle as possible.

Karen Kline looked shocked. "Oh, no!" she said quickly. "We've never had any trouble with Rachel at all." Her face became pale again. "I'm so afraid she's been kidnapped," she said, as though she was afraid even to speak the words. "Allen and I aren't rich, even though we live very well. All our money is tied up in the house. Someone must have gotten the idea that we could pay a king's ransom—"

Nancy touched Mrs. Kline's shoulder. "There's no reason to jump to conclusions. We have to wait to see if anyone calls or sends a ransom note," she said.

"I don't think she was kidnapped," Beth remarked slowly, staring at Rachel's dresser.

"Why?" Nancy asked.

Beth left her place beside Mrs. Kline to walk over to the bureau. The top was crowded with a jewelry chest, a music box, makeup, perfume, and a framed picture of Rachel with the rest of the cheerleading squad. "Because

Rachel's bank is empty," she said, excitement rising in her voice. She pointed at an expensive electronic bank on Rachel's dresser.

Mrs. Kline jumped up to see for herself. "You're right!" she said, holding up the bank. "And I know that she had taken money out of her account and was keeping it here. Now it's gone!"

Karen Kline dashed for the door. "Allen!" she cried out into the hall.

Nancy and Beth followed Mrs. Kline downstairs. While Mrs. Kline talked with her husband, Nancy and Beth joined the boys outside by the pool.

"Rachel must have run away," Beth announced. Then she explained about the missing money.

"But why would she have done that?" Josh wondered. "She seemed a little edgy this morning, but she's not the type of person to run away. She knows Mom and Dad love her."

"I'd like to question a few more of Rachel's friends," Nancy said thoughtfully, watching as sunlight danced in golden patches on the pool's cool blue water. "Somebody must know something."

"There's a party down at the Surf Club later," Beth put in helpfully. "Why don't you all come? That'll give you a chance to find out if anybody knows what's going on."

"Good idea," Nancy said, looking at her watch. "What time does it start?"

"Soon—at six," Beth answered. "But it'll go late. Bring your bathing suits. Everybody's planning on swimming after they've had dinner and danced for a while."

Josh and Ned agreed to attend the party, but they said they probably wouldn't feel like swimming. "I just hope Mr. and Mrs. Kline will be okay," Beth said in a faraway tone. "They don't deserve this."

Beth's words struck Nancy as odd. She was about to ask for an explanation when the girl glanced at her watch. "Well, I guess I'd better get home—my folks would like to see me before I take off. Catch you at the party."

"Right," said Ned.

"I guess I'll go inside and see if I can do anything to help my folks," Josh told them.

Ned pulled up two deck chairs for him and Nancy. "What do you think?" he asked after they were settled.

Nancy was staring at the clear California sky and frowning. "My guess is Rachel probably ran away," she said after a while. "She took her savings. On the other hand, why would she be in such a rush that she had to miss her own graduation? And why didn't she take her car?"

"I can't explain the graduation ceremony. But she doesn't need the car if she's with somebody else," Ned pointed out.

Nancy snapped her fingers. "You know, you're right. Someone like her boyfriend Dennis, for example."

Nancy explained what Beth had told her about Dennis.

"So you think they're together?" Ned asked.

"I don't know about that. But I do know one thing: this party should be very interesting."

"I recognize that look, Nancy," Ned said with a smile.

"What look?" Nancy asked.

"That look that says you're happy to be on a new case."

Promptly at six Nancy, Josh, and Ned left for the party in Rachel's car.

The Surf Club turned out to be a nice restaurant overlooking the beach. Tables were set up on the terrace, complete with colorful umbrellas. A band was playing the latest hits. Just beyond the terrace was a dance floor crowded with graduates and their dates determined to have a good time. Waiters in white coats were bustling around, setting out a buffet dinner on a long table back on the terrace.

While Josh and Ned went to get sodas, Nancy stood observing the crowd. Mike Rasmussen approached her almost immediately, bringing a pretty brown-haired girl with him. Nancy saw Beth coming toward them, too.

"I don't suppose anybody's heard anything from Rachel," Mike said, sounding almost testy.

Nancy supposed he was just concerned, like everybody else. "Nothing yet," she said.

"I'm Jessica Bates," the girl beside him announced. "And if you want my opinion, you're all wasting your time looking for Rachel. It's obvious that she's run off with her punk boyfriend, Dennis Harper," she finished smugly.

Mike glowered at Jessica, but before Nancy could ask her what she meant, Beth was beside her. She looked terrific in a green silk jumpsuit.

"I can't imagine why any of us would want your opinion," she said sweetly. "You don't like Rachel, and everybody knows it."

Jessica drew back, looking insulted. She started to say something, then stopped herself.

"I'm Nancy Drew," Nancy told her, since no one had introduced the two.

Jessica glared at Beth for a moment before lifting her chin and turning a smiling face on Nancy. "Welcome to Beverly Hills," she said. "I'm sure you'll find it's a very exciting place." With that, she turned and walked away, Mike following her to the buffet table.

"Still no news?" Beth asked, watching Nancy's face.

Nancy shook her head. "No news," she confirmed. "Tell me about Dennis Harper," Nancy said firmly as Ned and Josh joined them at one of the umbrella-covered tables.

For a moment fear flickered in Beth's eyes, but then she sighed and answered, "Rachel broke up with Mike about a month ago to date Dennis. He's kind of wild—Dennis, I mean. He graduated from Ocean Highlands last year."

"And?" Nancy prompted.

"Dennis works at a stereo equipment store in West Hollywood," Beth went on. "It's called Sound Performance. Mike works there, too."

Nancy glanced at Mike, who was standing in line at the buffet table next to Jessica. "He's not exactly crazy about Dennis, I take it."

Beth gave a nervous giggle and shook her head. "You've got that right," she agreed.

"Do my parents know about this Dennis

character?" Josh asked. "This is the first I've heard about him since I got back from school."

Beth shrugged. "I don't know what Rachel told your mom and dad," she said.

Ned was looking at the buffet table. "Let's eat," he suggested. "I'm starved."

The four of them got plates, but Ned was the only one who ate much. Nancy was eager to question some other kids to find out more about Rachel and Dennis Harper.

No one was eager to talk, though, and after another hour, Josh wanted to leave. He was understandably worried about his parents, and of course, he wanted to know if there had been any new developments. There was always the hope that Rachel had called or gone home while they were at the party.

"Are you going to start your internship tomorrow?" Ned asked Josh as the three of them headed for the parking lot.

Josh shrugged. "I'm not sure I could concentrate, knowing Rachel might be in trouble."

Nancy had already decided that their best chance of finding Rachel was to find Dennis. She decided to pay a visit to Sound Performance first thing in the morning.

They went to the Camaro and were about to get into the car when they noticed a piece of paper tucked under one of the windshield wipers. Nancy pulled it out and saw that it was a program for the Ocean Highlands High School graduation ceremony.

As her eyes scanned the page Nancy felt a rush of fear.

"Stop looking for Rachel or you may get hurt," someone had written in large black letters. "Love, The Kats."

Chapter

Four

Nancy handed the program to Josh. "Read this," she told him, her thoughts racing. Just who were these "Kats," and who was the note intended for? Were they threatening just her, or were Ned and Josh included? Was it just some prank, or could these Kats have something to do with Rachel's disappearance?

As Josh scanned the program Ned read it over his friend's shoulder. He gave a low whistle.

"I don't get it," Josh murmured. "Why are these Kats threatening us?"

Ned's expression was worried. "They obviously don't want us to find Rachel," he concluded, following Nancy's train of thought.

Nancy nodded. "That's what I decided, too," she told Josh. She took the program from him and read it again. "I do get notes like this all the time," she told Josh, to relieve his fears.

"And they haven't stopped you before," Ned pointed out ruefully.

With a smile, Nancy answered him. "You got that right, Nickerson. I'd say we have more reason than ever to find Rachel Kline."

The next morning Josh's parents convinced him to go to the movie studio. They promised they'd call if there was any news about Rachel. Mr. and Mrs. Kline were going to go to the police to convince them to file a missing persons report, then to the bank to find out if Rachel had closed out her savings account.

After dropping Josh off at the studio in Rachel's car, Ned and Nancy consulted a map and set out for Sound Performance.

It was a warm, sunny day with hardly any of the usual L.A. smog. As they drove along with the car windows open the wind felt good in Nancy's hair, and her spirits lifted. Finding out where Dennis worked was the best lead they had.

"I have a feeling that if we find Dennis Harper, we're going to be closer to finding Rachel."

"You think he kidnapped her?" Ned asked, keeping an eye out for their exit.

"I don't know," Nancy answered. "We don't have a ransom note." She thought for a moment. "Maybe they have run away. One thing's sure: Rachel's missing, and I overheard a conversation she had with Dennis that might involve him. Chances are they're together."

They found Sound Performance across the street from a large shopping mall. The building was a little run-down, and two of the neon letters in "Performance" were burned out. Inside, the store was crowded with merchandise, though, and there were a number of customers checking out the VCRs, camcorders, color TVs, and stereo systems.

A young salesman approached them immediately. "Welcome to Sound Performance," he said. "May I help you?"

Nancy hoped to spot Mike Rasmussen. She remembered Beth had told her he worked there, too. "We'd like to talk to the owner."

"You mean Mr. Lindenbaum?"

Nancy nodded. The salesman looked mildly disappointed but turned and pointed out a middle-aged man with a few strands of hair combed over his large bald spot. Mr. Lindenbaum, in pink slacks, an open-necked shirt, and a cardigan sweater that barely closed over his stomach, was busy selling a customer a new TV.

Nancy and Ned waited until he was finished before walking over to him.

"Mr. Lindenbaum?" Nancy held out her hand. "I'm Nancy Drew, and this is Ned Nickerson. We'd like to ask you a few questions.."

"Ralph Lindenbaum," he said with a smile. "Happy to be of service. What did you have in mind, a nice young couple like you?" His gaze shifted slightly to take in Ned. "A microwave? A VCR? We have both new and reconditioned appliances—"

"We'd like to talk to Dennis Harper," Nancy broke in politely, glancing around the store. "Is he here today?"

Ralph Lindenbaum looked decidedly less friendly. "What do you want with him?" He almost spat out the question.

"A friend of ours is missing," Ned answered, his hands resting on his hips. "Her name is Rachel Kline, and she and Dennis were dating."

Ralph scratched his head and carefully smoothed his hair back over the bald spot. "I could tell that kid was no good," he said. "Punk haircut and all. I'd heard he'd been in trouble before I hired him, too. Just thought I'd give him a chance." He paused to sigh dramatically. "Harper isn't around here anymore. I fired him day before yesterday, when some speakers turned up missing. It wasn't the first time things were missing when he worked. I made sure it was the last time, though!"

Nancy was worried. What if Dennis had stolen the equipment to have money to run off with Rachel? Or if he was a thief, there was a chance he could be a kidnapper, too. If that was the case, Rachel could be in serious danger.

She forced herself to stop thinking the worst. First they had to find out if Rachel was with him. "Can we have his telephone number, please?" she asked. "It's very important that we find him."

"This way," Ralph grumbled, turning and walking toward the back of the store. He rubbed the back of his neck with one hand as he moved. "Knew that boy was bad news," he muttered.

"Do you know Rachel Kline?" Ned asked.

"Never heard of her," Ralph mumbled, pushing open the door to a cluttered office. The desk was buried in invoices and telephone messages. "The police involved in this?" he asked, flipping through a small metal file box on a battered credenza.

"As of today, yes," Ned said. "Rachel's been missing since yesterday."

"Here it is," Ralph said, pulling a card and handing it to Nancy.

There was no address, just the name Dennis Harper, which was scrawled sloppily, and a phone number. Nancy copied it down in a notebook she always carried with her and handed the card back. "Do you know where Dennis lives?"

Ralph shook his head. "Sorry. Can't help you there."

"Thanks," Nancy said with a note of frustration. At least they had a telephone number. It was a start.

"No problem," Ralph answered. Then, with a shrug, he added, "You're probably going to find out that loser has left the country."

"I hope you're wrong," Nancy said, but she found that she was thinking the same thing. Still, there was no solid reason to suspect Dennis had kidnapped Rachel. "Thank you," she said, snapping her purse closed.

"Thanks," Ned added, holding the door open for Nancy. "Where to from here?" he asked once they were back outside.

"To the nearest telephone. We're going to give Dennis Harper a call."

Ned stopped at a fast-food restaurant and ordered sodas to go while Nancy went to the pay phone.

"No luck?" he asked, holding out a cup to her once she had returned.

Nancy shook her head. "Nobody answered."

Ned shrugged. "Maybe we had the wrong number. You said his handwriting was terrible," he said before taking a sip of his soda. "Maybe we should call directory assistance."

"Good idea." Nancy took another coin from her purse. "Be right back."

Nancy punched in the number for directory assistance and asked for Dennis's number. After a short pause, a recorded voice came on the line.

"I'm sorry. At the request of the subscriber, that number is unlisted."

Nancy hung up the receiver and drummed her fingers against the side of the phone booth. She let out a sigh and headed back to Ned.

"Strike out?" he asked, reading her face.

"Yep. Unlisted. We're back to square one."

"Look, Nancy," Ned said, putting his arms around her. "We'll find him—and her. I know we will. Let's head back to the Klines', have a swim, and put our heads together. A little sun may get us thinking more clearly."

Nancy smiled. Ned was good at reassuring her. "Okay. Maybe Rachel wrote down his address somewhere," she added. "We can check her room."

Nancy and Ned were back at the Klines' house before Mr. and Mrs. Kline. Ned headed upstairs while the maid told Nancy that they wouldn't be back until late that night. They were going to visit some of Rachel's friends' parents, and then there was a private party for some of the graduates and their parents.

"A party?" Nancy echoed, surprised.

"They think they might be able to learn something from Rachel's friends," she explained as she headed back to the kitchen. "You and Ned are invited, too. And I'm sure Josh will be going."

Remembering what little help Mike and Jessica had been the night before, Nancy doubted that Rachel's friends would tell her parents much. Still, there weren't many leads in the case, and they had to start somewhere.

"Nancy?" Ned came up to her in the hallway. "There's no address book. I just looked. I couldn't find a thing in Rachel's room with even Dennis's name on it. She really kept this guy a secret, didn't she?"

"It looks that way, but why?" Nancy asked. Before Ned could answer, the maid came back to tell them she'd set a late lunch by the pool for them.

"Thanks," Nancy said absently. "How about that swim, Nickerson? And how about a party later?"

When Nancy came downstairs that night dressed in a black tank top, roomy white overshirt, and black-and-white-checked miniskirt, Josh and Ned were standing at the foot of the stairs. Both let out whistles.

Nancy grinned. "You don't look so bad yourselves," she said, taking in Ned's red dress shirt and beige chinos. "Ready?"

The three of them set out for the party, which was being held in an ultramodern house perched on the side of one of the San Gabriel foothills. The place was surrounded by redwood decks, and the views of Los Angeles at dusk were spectacular.

Josh introduced Nancy and Ned to the host and hostess of the party, longtime friends of the Klines, and then he and Ned went off to get cold drinks.

Nancy was standing alone at the railing of the deck, thirty feet above the pool, which was full of shouting, laughing kids. As she watched the setting sun she felt sad, thinking that Rachel should be there, having fun and celebrating with her friends.

She heard someone behind her. "It's about time, Nickerson," she murmured without turning. "I was just thinking about enjoying the view with you."

She started to reach out for Ned. But before her hand moved a couple of inches, two strong hands struck her hard in the back. In the next instant she was sailing headfirst over the deck railing!

Chapter

Five

As she fell through the air Nancy reached out desperately for a handhold. Nothing. She was vaguely aware of the swimmers' screams and panic-stricken faces as she plummeted headfirst into the pool.

The water closed over her. Sinking quickly to the bottom, Nancy almost blacked out when her shoulder struck the concrete floor of the pool. The pain was intense. Gasping but trying not to swallow water, she propelled herself up to the surface.

When she finally bobbed up, she looked

around, and one of the first things she saw was Ned hurrying through the crowd toward her. Josh was close behind.

Nancy lifted her eyes to the terrace high overhead, but she knew it would be useless. The deck was empty. Whoever had pushed her was gone.

"Are you all right?" everyone asked at once, crowding around her.

Nancy nodded, realizing how lucky she'd been to land in the deep end of the pool instead of the shallow one. A bruised shoulder was hardly anything. "I'm fine. Did any of you see who pushed me?"

The swimmers glanced at one another and shook their heads. Until Nancy had actually fallen into the pool, they'd all been having too good a time to notice anything happening on a deck thirty feet above their heads.

Disappointed, Nancy kicked slowly to the side. Her clothes were heavy with water, but Ned was there with a hand extended to help her climb out.

"What happened?" he asked. "Are you hurt?"

"One question at a time," Nancy replied with a shaky smile, drying her face and pushing back her hair with a corner of a towel someone tossed to her. "I was standing up there on the deck, admiring the view, when I heard someone behind me. I thought it was you. The next thing I knew, someone had pushed me, and I was falling into the pool."

Karen and Allen Kline ran up just then with some of the other parents. Again Nancy explained what had happened.

Mrs. Becker, the hostess, offered Nancy a change of clothes. After Nancy had slipped into a pair of dry white shorts and a red T-shirt, she went back to the pool and joined the Klines and Josh and Ned. Allen Kline was in the middle of telling his son what little he and his wife had learned that day.

"So the police took the report, but they said there wasn't much they could do. At least not until there's a ransom note—if there is one." The fear in his voice was evident.

"There hadn't been any other recent withdrawals from her savings account," Karen Kline added in a bleak voice. "I just don't know what to think or even what to hope for."

"Don't worry, Mom," Josh told her. "We'll find her, or she'll probably come back on her own."

"Josh is right, Mrs. Kline," Ned offered. "The police will do what they can, and Nancy and I will do what we can, too."

Karen Kline gave Ned a small, warm smile.

"I'm really grateful for your help." She reached out for her husband's arm. "I'd like to go home now, Allen. If Rachel does call, I'd like one of us to answer instead of the maid."

Allen nodded sadly. "We're not accomplishing anything here," he agreed. "Good night, kids. Thanks for your help, and I'm sorry about your accident, Nancy."

Nancy managed a smile. "Don't worry about me. Please, before you go, could I just ask you a couple of questions about Dennis Harper?"

Mr. and Mrs. Kline seemed to become tense at the mention of Dennis's name. "Do you know him?" Nancy went on. Ned raised a hand ever so slightly, telling her to go easy.

"Not well," Mr. Kline answered after reflecting a moment. "He certainly isn't the kind of boy we'd expect Rachel to like. He's got one of those punk haircuts and a pretty tough attitude to match it."

Nancy explained that she and Ned were concentrating on locating him. "Do you have any idea where he lives?"

"You think Rachel's with him?" Josh asked before his mother could answer.

"Well, of course, we don't know," Ned explained. "Still, it may not be a coincidence that he's not around and Rachel's missing."

Deep furrows showed in Mrs. Kline's forehead. "You'd better tell the police to track him down, Allen."

"I'll do that right away," Mr. Kline agreed. "If she is with him, she could be in trouble. I knew we should never have let her go out with him!" With that, Allen Kline disappeared inside the house to use a telephone. Mrs. Kline and Josh quickly followed him.

Ned and Nancy remained at their poolside table. He turned to her. "Any idea who pushed you?" he asked.

"Not a clue," she said, laughing. "There's a pattern here, though. Whenever we're around Rachel's friends, someone tries to scare us off."

"What do you think it means?" Ned asked.

Before Nancy could answer, Beth, Jessica, and Mike came toward their table, towels slung around their necks. There was another guy with them, someone Nancy didn't recognize.

"This is Peter Henley," Beth said. "I don't think you've met him. Peter, this is Nancy Drew and Ned Nickerson. They're friends of Josh Kline's from school."

"Hi," Peter said with a smile as the four of them pulled up chairs and sat down at the table.

"Ned and I went to Sound Performance today, looking for Dennis," she said to Mike Rasmussen. "Sorry we missed you."

"I'm off a couple of days this week because of graduation," Mike replied.

"Mr. Lindenbaum said he fired Dennis because some stereo equipment turned up missing," Ned put in.

Mike looked at Beth, Jessica, and Peter before meeting Ned's gaze and nodding. "I'm not surprised," he said bitterly.

"What do you mean?" Nancy asked.

"You'd better tell them. It's all right. I know how you feel," Jessica said with a sigh.

For a moment Mike hesitated. Then he shrugged and muttered, "Okay." His eyes met Nancy's. "I was really in love with Rachel. Maybe I still am, a little. When she broke up with me to go out with Dennis, it hurt a lot. Then when I figured Harper was ripping off Sound Performance, I didn't know what to do. I wanted to tell Rachel, but I thought she wouldn't believe me."

"Why did you think he was stealing?" Nancy asked, leaning forward a little in her chair. "Did you see Dennis take something?"

Mike shook his head. "No—if I had, I would have turned him in. There were just coincidences. Also, he seemed to have a lot of money for a guy who worked part-time for minimum wage."

"Dennis is a jerk," Jessica said disdainfully, fiddling with the straw in her glass. "I think he's behind all these robberies."

"What robberies?" Nancy was quick to ask.

Peter joined the conversation. "Somebody's been ripping off houses in Beverly Hills lately," he said. "Expensive stuff like VCRs, video cameras, and equipment have been missing."

Beth was fiddling nervously with her pendant, a gold cat with white opals for eyes, and Nancy noticed she was a little pale. "Dennis always hung out at the Snake Pit," she put in. "It's a kind of crummy place downtown. Maybe that's where to look for him."

"Yeah, I'd see him there a lot when I was working," Peter added.

"You work there?" Ned asked.

"Sometimes. I like the music. The crowd's okay. An under-eighteen place. You know. No drinking, just music, video games, pinball, and fun." Peter slouched in his chair. "I never liked Dennis, though. He's a bit rough for that place."

"Do you think someone there might know where he is?" Nancy asked.

"I can think of a few people to ask," Peter offered.

Now we're getting somewhere, Nancy thought. "How about going now?"

"I'll go find Josh," Ned said with a nod of agreement, pushing back his chair.

Fifteen minutes later Nancy, Ned, and Josh were headed for the Snake Pit, following Mike, Beth, Jessica, and Peter. The club was in one of L.A.'s seedier areas, with a lot of empty warehouses.

"Some artists and musicians live down here," Josh explained. "It used to be dangerous, but now it's mostly trendy."

They met Rachel's friends in the club's parking lot, and Nancy took the lead. Her cases had taken her to worse places than this, she thought as she pushed open the heavy metal door.

The Snake Pit was full of smoke, and there were black leather jackets everywhere. The crowd—girls *and* guys—looked pretty tough.

Up on the stage a band hammered out earsplitting music. Nancy couldn't make out any of the words. Waitresses in vinyl miniskirts squeezed between packed tables, carrying trays of soft drinks.

"Does anybody see Dennis?" Nancy asked, raising her voice to be heard over the noise.

Jessica, Beth, and Mike shook their heads.

Peter was busy saying hello to someone he knew.

"It's early," Josh said, scanning the crowd.

"Is there anybody here you'd recognize as a friend of Dennis's?" Nancy asked.

"We don't hang around with this crowd," Jessica shouted just as the music died.

People at surrounding tables turned to stare at her, and the girl slipped down a little in her chair.

"Did my sister ever tell you she wanted to run off with this guy?" Josh asked Beth. "I mean, seeing this crowd he hung out with, I can't believe she would."

"No," Beth answered quickly, her eyes widening. "Of course not. I didn't even think she was all that serious about him."

"She was serious enough to dump me for the guy," Mike put in sadly.

"I don't know why you don't just forget her and start going out with somebody else," Jessica said coldly. Everyone stared at her in stunned surprise.

"Should we 'just forget' that Rachel is missing, too?" Mike demanded, his tone furious.

"If she's missing, it's her own choice!" Jessica spat out the words. "She and that boyfriend of hers are probably in Mexico somewhere, laughing at all of us!"

"Arguing won't get us anywhere," Ned said, interceding quietly.

Beth was shifting around in her chair, her eyes moving anxiously over the crowd. Once again, she was fingering the little gold cat on her necklace. "I think we should get out of here," she said with a shiver. "This place gives me the creeps."

Just then Mike leapt out of his chair, nearly toppling the sodas off the table.

"What's got into you?" Jessica asked, moving out of his way.

"There's Dennis!" he shouted, pointing past the stage.

Nancy jumped up and looked in the direction Mike was pointing. Before she could catch a glimpse of Dennis, though, the lights went off and the whole club went black.

Chapter

Six

Nancy reached under the table for her purse. She rummaged inside, pulled out her penlight, and pointed it in the direction Dennis had taken.

Even in its dim light, though, Nancy could see that the boy had disappeared. Mike was standing by the edge of the stage, and Ned and Josh were next to her.

When the lights came back up again a few seconds later, Mike took off in the direction where Dennis had disappeared. Nancy, Ned, and Josh were right behind him. They pushed their way through the crowd, back by the club's dressing rooms, and outside. Nancy's first instincts were right, though. Dennis appeared to be gone.

In the parking lot Mike shoved a hand through his hair and sighed.

"We've lost him."

"Maybe he doubled back and is inside," Nancy suggested.

"I don't think so. We all saw him take off this way," Ned pointed out. "He's not here."

Nancy didn't like giving up, especially when they'd come so close to finding Dennis.

"We can look around inside," Mike agreed, "but I don't think we're going to find him."

Back inside the club, Nancy and the others looked for any sign of Dennis. Ned went off in one direction while Mike and Josh checked out the dancers and people sitting at tables in another direction.

When they all met back at their table, Beth asked Mike if he'd found anyone who'd seen Dennis.

"Nope. We struck out," Mike said with a frown.

Peter Henley came by just then. Nancy asked him if he'd spotted Dennis around the club.

Peter shook his head. "If he was here, I

didn't see him," he said. With that, he went off to dance with a girl with bleached blond hair and spiked black boots.

"We might as well get out of here," Mike told Jessica and Beth. "We're wasting our time."

"It took you long enough to figure that out," Jessica muttered. She and Beth both seemed relieved as they got to their feet.

"Coming?" Mike asked Nancy, Ned, and Josh.

"I think we'll stick around for a while," Josh said.

Mike shrugged. "Good luck," he replied. He, Jessica, and Beth hurried out of the club after asking Peter if he wanted a ride home. He shook his head no and continued dancing.

"What do you think Dennis was doing here?" Ned asked when the three of them were alone.

"My guess is he came to talk to someone," Nancy offered, her eyes scanning the crowd. "From the way he took off when he saw Mike, it didn't seem like he was here to have a good time."

"Should we start asking around to see if anyone here knows Dennis or Rachel?" Ned wanted to know when the three of them were alone at the table.

"Sounds good to me," Josh answered. "Nancy, you'd better stick with one of us."

Ned's eyes sparkled as he watched Nancy react to Josh's innocent remark.

"I'll be fine on my own," she said pointedly.

Josh looked at her in surprise, then a grin broke out across his face. "Sure. Sorry, Nancy."

She smiled. "No problem. How about if you guys take opposite sides of the room while I cover the middle?"

Ned gave her a salute. "Yes, ma'am," he said.

Nancy drew a deep breath and approached a table where eight people were sitting. She looked as friendly as possible. "Hi, I'm looking for Dennis Harper, and I was wondering if any of you know him."

Eight pairs of eyes turned up to her face. Eight pairs of suspicious eyes. None of them seemed to recognize Dennis's name.

"Why do you ask?" inquired one girl.

"I've got some questions to ask him."

The girl's gaze took in Nancy's shorts and T-shirt with distaste. "You a cop?"

"Don't be an idiot, Marcy," put in one of the guys at the table. "She's too young to be a cop."

"Maybe," said Marcy.

"I'm just a friend," Nancy told them.

Marcy's eyebrows rose. "Of Dennis's?"

"Of Rachel Kline's, actually."

The band launched into a throbbing beat, and most of the kids got up to dance, but Marcy and another guy stayed behind. Marcy appeared very curious. "Is Dennis in any trouble?"

"Maybe," Nancy said, sitting down in an empty chair and ignoring the stare from the guy with Marcy. "Did you know Rachel's missing?"

Marcy wouldn't meet Nancy's eyes. "Rachel Kline." She said the name with a touch of scorn. Nancy was sure that Marcy knew Rachel, whether she'd admit it or not. "Are her parents blaming Dennis?"

Nancy shrugged. "Nobody's blaming anybody. Rachel's family is really worried, of course. We're just trying to find her—and him."

"Dennis was in here earlier," Marcy confessed reluctantly. "But he's gone now."

"Do you know what he was doing here?"

Marcy pulled back at the question. "No," she said. She turned to start talking to the guy at the table.

"It could be important," Nancy pressed gently.

At that moment the guy interrupted. "Let's dance," he said to Marcy, wrenching her out of her chair. It was clear he thought she'd said too much as it was.

During the next half hour every person Nancy talked to denied knowing Rachel and claimed not to have seen Dennis that night.

Ned joined her as she left the last table. "No luck," he said, spreading his hands. "I even tried the guys in the band, and Josh talked to the kitchen crew and the waitresses. If anybody here has ever heard of Harper, he's not admitting it."

Nancy nodded. "I came up dry, too. What do you say we get out of here? I'm getting a headache."

"Let's find Josh," he agreed, taking Nancy's hand and pushing a path through the crowd.

As they were leaving Nancy noticed something scrawled on the wall beside the front door and stopped for a closer look. There, among the phone numbers, names, and other graffiti, was a drawing of a cat with white eyes.

It looked familiar, but Nancy didn't know why until they were outside, where it was quieter, and the evening air was pleasantly cool. Beth Hanford came into her mind, and Nancy remembered the necklace she'd been wearing at the party earlier that evening—a gold cat with white opal eyes.

She caught Ned's arm and pulled him back inside. "Look at this," she said, pointing at the cat. "Doesn't it look familiar to you?"

Ned thought for a moment, then nodded. "Beth was wearing a necklace like that," he said.

Nancy frowned as they went back outside to catch up with Josh. "It probably doesn't mean anything," she mused. "Still, it's an odd coincidence."

Nobody said much on the way back to Beverly Hills—each was lost in his or her own thoughts. Where could Rachel be? Was she safe? If Dennis *had* kidnapped her, why hadn't he sent a ransom note? And what had he been doing in the club that night? It seemed like a pretty big risk for him to be seen in public if he had anything to do with Rachel's disappearance.

The house was all lit up when they arrived at the Klines', and there was a police car in the driveway. Nancy's heart started pounding. She hoped the police had brought good news. She hurried into the house behind Josh and Ned.

"Mom!" Josh yelled the moment they were through the front door. "Dad! Where is everybody?"

Karen Kline appeared at the top of the grand, curving stairway. "Up here, dear," she said, her voice shaky.

"What's going on?" Josh demanded, racing up the stairs. "Did they find Rachel?"

Slowly Mrs. Kline shook her head. "No," she said. Then, without saying anything more, she walked down the hallway, moving as if she was in a daze.

Josh followed her at top speed, and Nancy and Ned came behind him at a slightly slower pace. It was obvious that something shattering had happened, and they didn't want to intrude.

Ned took Nancy's hand and gave it a slight squeeze. The light was on in Rachel's room, and they could hear Mr. Kline speaking in an angry, agitated voice.

Mrs. Kline explained to Josh as Mr. Kline talked with a police officer. "When we got home, we checked to see if your sister was back. This is what we found."

Pausing at Rachel's doorway just then, Nancy gasped.

Rachel's room had been ransacked!

Chapter

Seven

EVERY DRESSER DRAWER had been emptied onto the floor, and the contents of the closet and bookcase were scattered everywhere. Even the mattress and box spring had been torn from the bed.

Nancy noticed a video camera lying on the floor in the corner. There were tapes scattered all around it.

"Take a look at this," she said, heading for the camera and bending down to get a closer look. In that moment Nancy ruled out burglary—the rest of the house was apparently untouched, and no thief would have left such an expensive camera behind.

Josh nodded. He was acting worried and distracted. "Rachel's interested in filmmaking, too," he said absently.

"I don't think it was a burglary, Mr. Kline," the police officer said as Rachel's father walked him out.

"Nothing's missing?" Nancy wanted to know as she went to stand at Mrs. Kline's side.

"Not as far as I can tell," Karen Kline answered. "Not even my jewelry." Nancy could see that she was on the verge of tears. "And I don't think we surprised whoever it was, either," the woman went on. "I mean, we didn't see anyone leaving the house. It had to have happened while we were still at the party."

"A burglar wouldn't have left without that camera," Ned said, voicing Nancy's conclusion. "Not to mention the rest of the stuff in the house."

"How could anyone get past the housekeeper? She should have heard a noise," Nancy said.

"Mrs. Morgan is a very sound sleeper, and her rooms are at the far end of the house. She also forgot to set the burglar alarm before going to sleep, so the intruder had no problems getting in and back out," Mrs. Kline answered with a slight shrug of her shoulders.

Nancy went back to the videotapes and studied them carefully. All had obviously been labeled by Rachel, with titles like "Day at the Beach," "Girls at the Mall," and "Boys Worth Watching." Nancy smiled sadly and turned back to the others. "Are the police going to dust for fingerprints?" she asked.

"I don't know how much good it will do," Mrs. Kline replied. "Allen and I touched lots of things while we were looking to see if anything was missing. The officer also said it wouldn't help unless whoever broke in had a prior record."

"Still," Nancy said, "fingerprints might offer an important clue. Suppose the culprit *does* have a record?"

Mrs. Kline nodded distractedly. "I'll ask Allen to speak to the police," she said, and she hurried out.

"Let's go talk," Josh said after a long sigh. Nancy nodded, and she and Ned followed him out of Rachel's room.

After Mr. and Mrs. Kline went off to bed, Josh, Ned, and Nancy sat down in the den with glasses of lemonade and a bowl of chips.

"It's been a long day," Josh said, rubbing his eyes. "And a confusing one. I just don't understand what's happening."

"Whoever broke in tonight was looking for something very specific," Nancy offered. Ned nodded his silent agreement. "But what?"

"The only thing we know for certain is that it must be connected to Rachel," Ned said. "And maybe also that it was something that could explain where she is now."

"Maybe." Nancy thought for a moment. "But we wouldn't know what the connection was."

"Here's another question: Who pushed you over the deck tonight, and why?" Josh asked.

Nancy shrugged. "Someone in Rachel's crowd who doesn't want us to find her, that's my guess."

"Could it have been Dennis?" Ned wondered.

"I doubt it," Nancy said firmly. "Judging from the way he ran out of the Snake Pit tonight, I don't think he'd risk being seen at a party."

Josh stood up. "I can't think anymore tonight, that's for sure. If you have time tomorrow, come by the studio and we can talk. My mom and dad are making me go to work every day. They think it's best if we try to stick to our normal routine."

Nancy smiled. "I agree with them."

After Josh went up to bed, Ned reached out to give Nancy a kiss. "Alone at last," he murmured into her hair.

"Don't worry, Nickerson," Nancy told him with a laugh. "You'll have me all to yourself tomorrow."

"Why? What happens tomorrow?" Ned asked curiously.

"Tomorrow we're going to track down Dennis Harper. No matter what."

As soon as Nancy got up the next morning she tried Dennis's phone number for what seemed like the fiftieth time. Still no answer. After quickly dressing in white slacks and a roomy blue cotton shirt, she hurried downstairs.

Josh, Ned, and the Klines were already in the dining room. The doorbell rang almost as soon as Nancy sat down at the table.

"That must be Lieutenant Heller," Mr. Kline said, getting up to answer the door himself. "The police promised to bring a fingerprint expert."

Everyone left the table to follow the two people upstairs to Rachel's room. The fingerprint woman sighed when she saw the mess the intruder had left. Fingerprints would be almost impossible to lift.

"I checked with your neighbors last night," the lieutenant said. "None of them saw or heard anything out of the ordinary while you were out."

"And nothing is missing," Mrs. Kline added. "We double-checked everything."

"Are there any leads on my daughter, Lieutenant?" Mr. Kline asked. "Have you been able to locate her boyfriend, Dennis?"

Lieutenant Heller raised his hands in a helpless gesture. "No leads, I'm afraid, Mr. Kline. But I do have an address for the Harper boy, and we're checking up on him."

Nancy's heart started to race. So the police knew where Dennis Harper lived. "Could you give me his address, Lieutenant?" she asked.

At the lieutenant's quizzical expression, Karen Kline explained that Nancy was an amateur detective and that she was helping them find their daughter.

"Hey, I've heard of you," Heller said with a smile. "I read about you in a paper somewhere. What do you know—Drew's your name, right?"

Nancy blushed, and Ned gave her a little poke in the ribs. "That's right. Could you give me Dennis's address? I'd like to check his place out."

The detective pulled a notebook from his shirt pocket, flipped it open, and read off an address. Nancy made a note of it and thanked the lieutenant.

"You won't be able to get in—unless he's there," he said, closing the notebook and tucking it away again. "And if he is there, he probably won't let you in. I can tell you that we went over that apartment with a fine-tooth comb and came up blank."

Nancy nodded. She still wanted to go out there herself. She'd ask Josh if they could borrow Rachel's car to drive out to Dennis's place.

Josh glanced at his watch. "I'm going to be late for work if I don't leave right now," he said, his tone apologetic. "If you guys want to use the car, you can drive me to work and take it," he said, reading Nancy's mind.

"Go ahead, Josh," Mr. Kline urged. "Try to have a good day."

Nancy lingered for just a moment after Josh and Ned went out, talking with Lieutenant Heller. "I understand there've been a lot of other break-ins in the community lately," she said.

Heller answered her as if she were a colleague. "Yes," he said with a nod. "There have been, and we've been getting nowhere with them."

"Just as you're getting nowhere finding our daughter," Mrs. Kline put in, sounding a little peevish.

The lieutenant's strong but ordinary face showed compassion as he met Karen's gaze. "We're trying, Mrs. Kline," he said quietly. "But the unfortunate truth is, we're swamped with reports of missing teenagers. It's an epidemic."

"Nancy!" Ned's voice called to her good-naturedly, from a distance.

"I'd like to talk to you again soon," Nancy said to the lieutenant.

He nodded and handed her his card. "Take care, Ms. Drew. We may be dealing with some very dangerous people. Please be careful."

Just as Nancy reached the bottom of the stairway the telephone rang. Mrs. Morgan answered it and held out the receiver of the hallway extension. "It's for you, Nancy," she said.

Nancy was surprised. "Hello?"

"Nancy, this is Beth Hanford." Beth sounded scared and anxious. "I need to talk to you. In person."

"I was just going out," Nancy answered,

conscious that Ned and Josh were waiting. She didn't want Josh to be late for his job because of her. "Could we meet later?"

"Twelve o'clock," Beth said. "The pizza place in the Golden Hills Mall?"

"I'll be there," Nancy promised after Beth gave her directions.

Nancy hung up and dashed out to catch up with Josh and Ned. The three of them got into the Camaro and headed for the movie studio.

"I hope they get a break in this case soon," Josh said as he maneuvered the sporty car through the early-morning traffic. "I don't think my folks—or I—can take much more."

Nancy and Ned were silent. There was nothing either of them could say to help.

When they reached the studio gates Josh's mood improved. It was obvious to Nancy that he loved his job after only one day. He gave a cheerful hello to the guard who checked his ID, and he asked for one-day passes for Nancy and Ned. Driving through the lot, they passed people dressed in costumes from every period.

"Visitors can come onto the lot on the other side if they buy a ticket," Josh explained. "They're not supposed to wander into this part, but it does happen sometimes."

Josh passed a lot of expensive cars to park the Camaro among some older, battered models. "Why don't you come over and look around for a couple of hours? A change from the case might do you some good," Josh said.

Nancy and Ned nodded their agreement, and Nancy said, "Just for an hour. We've got lots to do." She was interrupted just then by a screech of tires and a loud crash.

Josh chuckled. "Don't worry, Nancy," he said. "It's just a scene being shot."

They wandered over to the set where Josh was working. An outdoor scene was being blocked, and Nancy and Ned found places to stand and watch where they were out of the way. Josh was already at work helping the assistant director's assistant.

"We'll only stay for a little while because I want to check out the address Lieutenant Heller gave me for Dennis Harper," Nancy explained. Then she filled him in on her appointment with Beth. "All right with you?" she asked.

"You bet." They were silent for a few minutes. "It'll be weird to sit in a theater and watch this," Ned whispered after a couple of minutes. Nancy's mind was mostly on the case she was trying to solve, but she did manage to smile and nod.

Ned appeared to be fascinated watching the hero of the movie—a well-known star—

rehearse. The actor jumped out of one car, leaving the door open behind him, and dragged a man out of another car parked nearby.

Nancy's mind wandered more and more until finally she knew she couldn't stay there another minute.

Josh had wandered off, and Nancy and Ned were looking for him so they could pick up his car keys. They were wandering behind the set when Nancy heard the roar of a car's engine behind them. She turned to look back and gripped Ned's hand.

In the next instant her heart jumped into her throat. A green sports car with tinted windows was bearing down on them at top speed! In another second they'd be run over!

Chapter

Eight

NANCY DIDN'T WASTE TIME talking. She dived to her right, pulling Ned with her. Belly-flopping onto the hard-packed earth, they rolled out of the car's path just as its wheels flew past, sending out sprays of dirt. The right tires missed them by no more than a foot.

"Are you hurt?" Ned asked, helping Nancy up.

"No," she said breathlessly. "Come on!" Her eyes were riveted on the car as it disappeared around a corner.

She and Ned took off after the car at a dead run. They had to get a glimpse of the driver.

When they made it around the corner, they found the car abandoned, with the door on the driver's side hanging open.

Josh and a couple of other crew members wandered toward them from the direction of their set.

"What happened?" Josh asked, seeing how filthy they both were.

Nancy was still checking for any sign of the driver, even though she knew it was probably hopeless. Whoever had tried to run them down was long gone.

"Somebody tried to kill us," Ned explained. "Fortunately Nancy saw them coming, and we rolled out of the way just in time."

"I'll call studio security," a guy in a plaid shirt called out. Another guy went to inspect the car.

"This is getting pretty heavy," Josh said, standing beside Ned and Nancy. "Somebody's playing hardball now."

"Maybe we can get a lead from the license-plate number," Nancy said hopefully.

Josh shook his head. "It's a studio car— we're using it in the movie. Whoever wanted to run you down must have ripped it off when the prop people were busy."

Within a couple of minutes a man and woman in security officers' uniforms arrived.

"What happened?" the woman asked.

Nancy explained that she and Ned had been walking along when someone tried to run them down, and the man in the jeans and plaid shirt told how the vehicle had been stolen from the property lot a few minutes earlier. Unfortunately, no one had seen anything.

"I think we should let Lieutenant Heller know about this," Josh said. He was pale under his suntan. "You two could have been killed."

Ned put an arm around Nancy and gave her a quick squeeze as he tried to reassure his friend. "We're okay," he said quietly.

The security people left, telling them there wasn't much they could do without a description. Nancy kicked herself for not having gotten a better look at the driver.

Finally a man in a baseball cap called out, "All right, everybody! Back to work. We've got a picture to shoot!"

Josh was reluctant to leave Nancy and Ned. "I'd better go," he said. "Maybe you two should get out of here before something else happens."

Nancy glanced at her watch. "Could we take your car now, Josh?" she asked. "We'll pick you up later."

"Sure," he answered, tossing the keys to

Ned. Then, with a slight wave, he turned and followed the others back to the movie set.

"I think we'd better go change," Ned said, looking down at his dusty clothes. Nancy's were even worse, since she had put on white slacks that morning.

"Me, too," she said.

"You're sure you're okay?" Ned asked as they walked through the lot to where Josh's car was parked.

Nancy gave him a squeeze. "I'm fine, Nickerson. How about you? You hit the ground just as hard as I did."

Ned grinned. "I'll live. Though it has occurred to me that hanging around with you might not be the best way to have a long and happy life."

Nancy chuckled, but then her expression turned serious. "Any idea who it was?"

Ned's grin had faded into an angry frown. "Don't know. Maybe the same person who shoved you off the deck at the party," he answered.

They'd reached Josh's car, and Ned opened the passenger door for Nancy. "One thing's sure—we had to have been followed from the Klines'," Nancy pointed out as she slipped into the car.

"You're right," Ned agreed, starting the

ignition. He turned to face her. "Nancy, maybe we should think about dropping this. The police are on the case. Whoever this person is, he or she is dead serious."

"You know I don't walk away from a case until it's solved," Nancy pointed out. "And it wasn't necessarily the same person who pushed me. There could be several people involved."

"If you had been hurt—"

"But I wasn't, Ned. And neither were you. Look, we're not stopping until we find Rachel and figure out what's going on."

"I just hope we survive that long," Ned said, pulling out of the parking lot.

When the two of them arrived back at the house less than a half hour later, Mrs. Kline greeted them at the door.

"My goodness," she exclaimed, taking in their clothes. "What happened?"

Nancy didn't want to alarm the woman, but she couldn't tell a lie, either. "There was an accident at the studio," she said. "But no one was hurt."

Mrs. Kline's eyes were wide with worry. "What kind of accident?"

Nancy glanced at Ned before reluctantly replying, "We were almost run down by a car."

Josh's mother gasped. "What?"

"Apparently somebody wants us to stop asking questions," Ned said quietly.

"Which means we might be getting close," Nancy added. "Mrs. Kline, have you heard anything from the police about the finger-prints?"

Even before Karen answered, Nancy could tell by her expression that the news was disap-pointing. "They did find a set of strange prints," she said. "But whoever broke in has no criminal record, so nobody can be identi-fied."

Nancy sighed. "I'm sorry," she said. "I take it there hasn't been any other news?"

Mrs. Kline shook her head, and her eyes moved over Nancy's and Ned's clothes again. "Maybe you should just let the police handle this. Allen and I would never forgive ourselves if something happened—"

"We've had experience with situations like this," Nancy broke in gently, squeezing Mrs. Kline's hand. "And I promise we'll be care-ful."

With that, Nancy and Ned excused them-selves and went upstairs. Once in her room, Nancy washed and changed into a pair of blue cotton shorts and a matching top. Downstairs,

Nancy found Ned waiting to go to the Golden Hills Mall to meet Beth. Dennis's apartment would have to wait until later.

Once they were in the car and headed toward the mall, Ned glanced over at Nancy quickly as he steered the car onto the highway.

"What do you think Beth wants to see you about?" he asked.

"Something about Dennis's relationship with Rachel, I hope," Nancy replied. The two were silent until Ned parked the car and the two of them headed to the cool, glass-topped shopping plaza.

After consulting a directory, Nancy and Ned found the colorful sign over the door of the pizza place.

"Do you want to talk to her alone?" Ned asked. He thought Beth would probably feel uncomfortable opening up with him there.

Nancy shook her head. "She sounded pretty anxious on the telephone this morning. Whatever it is, she's having a lot of trouble holding it in."

They entered the restaurant, and Nancy spotted Beth in a corner of the room. Jessica was standing beside the table, her hands thrust into the pockets of her jean jacket. She didn't look friendly.

Nancy and Ned approached as quietly as they could.

"You'd just better not spill the beans, Hanford," Jessica was warning an ashen-faced Beth in acid tones. "Because if you do, you'll pay for it!"

Chapter

Nine

WHEN SHE TURNED AROUND and faced Nancy and Ned, Jessica's cheeks were glowing with color. The girl took one hand out of her jacket pocket to push her hair back, and a piece of paper slipped to the floor.

"Spill what beans?" Nancy challenged Jessica. It was obvious to Nancy that she had overheard something important. She wasn't going to let Jessica off.

Jessica and Beth were both caught off guard. Beth's face was white, but Jessica had recovered quickly. "You know, Nancy," Jessica said tartly, "I'm getting a little tired of all your questions. It just so happens that what Beth and I were talking about is none of your business."

Beth bit down hard on her lower lip, then bolted out of her seat. "I can't talk to you now, Nancy," she said hurriedly. "Sorry!"

Before Nancy could think of a way to stop her, Beth raced out of the restaurant without a backward glance.

Nancy folded her arms and turned to Jessica, who raised her chin a degree and stared defiantly into Nancy's face. Nancy wouldn't let Jessica get away.

"I'll get some sodas," Ned said, and he went over to the counter.

"Sit down, Jessica," Nancy said. She could tell the girl was hiding something, and she was determined to find out what.

Jessica shook her head. She pushed back her brown hair again and gave Nancy a steely stare from her icy blue eyes. "Why should I?" she asked with a smirk.

"Whatever you said really scared Beth," Nancy began.

Jessica shrugged. "Beth is a wimp," she said.

Nancy thought about the fall she'd taken from the Beckers' deck and the near miss on the studio lot that day. She wondered if Jessica could have been behind one or both attacks.

The girl seemed to be good at threatening people, and it was only one step further to actually endangering a life. She confronted the girl.

"You know, Jessica," she said, "whatever it is you're hiding, I'm going to find out. And if you're involved with Rachel's disappearance, the charges might be very serious."

A shocked expression passed over Jessica's face, but she quickly composed herself. When she spoke, her words were harsh and bitter. "Rachel deserves whatever she gets," she said. With that, she stormed toward the door, almost knocking down Ned, who was carrying three sodas on a tray.

Jessica *is* hiding something, Nancy thought. She didn't even try to defend herself. Quickly Nancy went over and retrieved the piece of paper that had fallen from Jessica's pocket. She hadn't wanted Jessica to see her pick it up.

"What happened?" Ned asked, setting down the tray and glancing over Nancy's shoulder as her eyes scanned the note.

On the front of the paper was a sketch of the cat she and Ned had seen on Beth's necklace and on the wall at the Snake Pit. "'Special party at Kat Club Headquarters,'" she read out loud. "'Four twenty-two Beach Drive. Seven P.M.'"

"When is it?" Ned asked.

"It's tomorrow night." She tapped the cat drawing with her fingernail. "I have a feeling we're about to make a major breakthrough."

Ned pushed one of the sodas toward Nancy and sat down opposite her. "Did you find out anything from Miss Personality?"

Nancy sighed. "No. And there's probably no use in trying to talk with Beth, either. Jessica really intimidated her. After we leave here, let's go to Dennis Harper's apartment."

Ned narrowed his eyes. "I don't think that's such a good idea, Nan. After everything that's happened, I think we should let the police handle Harper."

"But—"

"Look, he could be the one who's been trying to scare you away. Maybe he knows you're on to him. He could be laying a trap for you right now."

Nancy had to admit that Ned had a point. Dennis Harper could be dangerous. "How about if we go later with Josh?" she asked. "With three of us, we should be safe."

"You don't let up, do you?" Ned said in mock exasperation. Nancy shook her head. "But now I think an afternoon in the sun beside the Klines' pool won't hurt, either," Ned suggested.

Breaking out in a wide grin, Nancy offered her hand for a shake. "It's a deal," she said.

When they arrived at the Klines', Allen Kline wasn't at home. He had forced himself to go to his office for the afternoon. Mrs. Kline was speaking to the police on the telephone. She shook her head, indicating that there were no new developments, so Nancy and Ned went upstairs to change.

Fifteen minutes later they were sitting with their feet dangling in the Klines' pool. "Not one word about the case," Ned said, laying a finger to Nancy's lips just as she was about to open her mouth.

She slipped into the water and swam out to the middle. Ned took a plunge off the diving board. While they were swimming, Nancy forced herself not to think about the case once. By the time they were drying off, her mind was clearer.

"I guess we'd better get Josh," Ned said, touching Nancy's cheek briefly with one finger. "You know, Nan, I wish we could be together like this more often."

Nancy nodded and studied her handsome boyfriend. What other guy could make her laugh and would help her out on cases the way he did? Nancy reached up and threw her arms around his neck as Ned wrapped his arms around her waist. She looked up into his warm brown eyes and was drawn closer to him. Before she knew it, they were caught in a breathtaking kiss that seemed to last forever.

"Wow," Ned murmured when it was over. "I love you, Nancy."

"I love you, too, Ned," Nancy said into Ned's ear. Reluctantly she pulled away and met his eye. "We'd better get going. I think Josh would resent having to walk all the way home."

As they headed to the studio ten minutes later traffic was especially heavy. Nancy and Ned were a few minutes late to pick Josh up at the studio gates. He appeared to be tired and discouraged.

"Any word?" he asked as they drove away.

Ned was still at the wheel. "Sorry, buddy," he said sympathetically. "As far as we know, there haven't been any new developments."

"We did find out about something called the Kat Club," Nancy told him. "They're having a party tomorrow night, and Ned and I are planning to crash it. Want to come along?"

Josh was frowning. "The Kat Club?"

Nancy reminded him about the threatening note they'd gotten the night of the party at the

Surf Club. "These Kats, whoever they are, don't want us around. Crashing their party is the best way to find out just who they are."

When they arrived back at the Kline house, Mrs. Morgan told them Mr. and Mrs. Kline were having dinner in their room. No one needed to say how difficult the last few days had been for them.

"I hope they'll let us know if there's anything we can do to help," Nancy said. "Josh, I want to ask you a favor—"

Just then the phone rang, and Nancy and Ned paused while Josh answered it. As he was hanging up he gave them a weary smile. "That was the studio. I have to go back to work for a few hours."

After Josh left, Ned said, "You're disappointed we can't go to Harper's place, aren't you?"

Nancy nodded. "But I guess it can wait. First thing tomorrow, though, right?"

"Right. Now how about—"

Mrs. Morgan came to find them. "Dinner is ready," she told them. "If you don't mind, I've set the table in the kitchen."

"Thanks, Mrs. Morgan," Nancy said.

"I'm starved," Ned said.

"What else is new?" Nancy replied, giving him a friendly punch in the side.

In the kitchen crisp seafood salads and warm rolls waited for them. Ned took a couple of sodas from the refrigerator and filled both their glasses.

Nancy sat down and picked up her fork. Through the kitchen windows she could see the swimming pool sparkling turquoise in the early-evening summer sun. She let her mind wander, chewing thoughtfully. "I think I'll call Beth later," she said after a while. "Maybe she's ready to talk now."

"I wouldn't bet on it," Ned answered, breaking a roll apart and buttering it generously. "It looked to me like Jessica scared her but good," he said.

"About what, that's the question," Nancy said. "What if she knows where Rachel is, and Jessica was warning her not to tell?"

"That doesn't make any sense," Ned said, pushing back his plate. "Why would Jessica not want us to find Rachel?"

"I don't know," Nancy admitted. "It is a little confusing. If Beth is really Rachel's friend, she'd find some way to let us know where she is."

"I'd say so," Ned agreed. "We still don't know how this Harper guy is involved," he pointed out.

"Jessica seems to think they've run off together," Nancy said. "Still, if that were the case, I think Rachel would have called her parents by now to let them know she was safe."

"What do you say we try to watch a movie on the VCR?" Ned suggested.

Reluctantly Nancy agreed. There was nothing more for her to do that night. Nancy and Ned rinsed their plates and cups and set them in the dishwasher. Then Ned took two cans of soda from the refrigerator, and they headed to the den.

Nancy looked at the tapes lying beside the VCR. She smiled when she saw *Casablanca,* one of her favorite old movies. "Can you stand it again?" she asked Ned. He smiled and then switched on the big-screen TV after slipping the tape into the VCR.

Ned settled himself on the couch next to Nancy, head back, arms folded across his chest. They waited, but nothing came on the screen. Frowning, Nancy got up and took the tape out. "Somebody must have erased it or something," she said. She put the tape aside and picked out another one.

She popped it into the machine. Almost immediately a famous mystery movie lit up the screen. Nancy settled down beside Ned again, and his arm came to rest comfortably around her shoulders.

Midway through the movie, the telephone rang. Knowing Mrs. Morgan was off for the night, Nancy answered it after only two rings.

"Kline residence," she said. From the other end Nancy could hear a low, rhythmic roar that sounded like the ocean.

"This is Rachel Kline," the caller said in a soft voice that Nancy recognized. "Could I please speak to my mom and dad?"

Chapter

Ten

DON'T HANG UP, RACHEL!" Nancy cried out. She signaled Ned, who bounded off the couch and out of the room at the sound of the girl's name. "We'll put your parents on right away."

"Okay," Rachel answered in a small voice. "But please hurry. I don't have much time."

"Where are you?" Nancy asked softly. "Are you all right?"

"I can't answer your questions," Rachel replied. She sounded as though she was about to burst into tears. "I'm just calling because I know my mom and dad must be awfully worried."

"We can help you," Nancy continued persuasively. "But first we need to know where you are."

"Rachel!" Karen Kline's frantic voice came on the line. "Rachel, honey—"

Feeling awkward about intruding, Nancy quietly hung up the receiver. Ned came rushing back into the room while she was rewinding the movie they'd been watching and putting it back into its case.

"Did she tell you anything?" he asked expectantly.

Nancy turned and shook her head as she met his eyes. "No, but she sounded really scared, and she said she didn't have much time."

Ned put his arms around Nancy. "At least we know she's okay," he said.

Nancy was about to give Ned a hug when Karen Kline came running into the room in her robe, followed by her husband.

"She hung up!" Rachel's mother cried, hugging her arms around her chest. "I was so close to finding out where she was when the line went dead!"

Allen Kline tried to comfort his wife. "At least we know she's alive."

"Did you hear anything in the background before she hung up?" Nancy prodded. "Any other voices?"

"No voices." Karen Kline paused, thinking. "There was a low murmuring—"

"The ocean," Nancy said. "I recognized it as soon as I picked up the phone," she explained.

Allen Kline's expression brightened. "Rachel must be somewhere close to the water."

"But where?" Mrs. Kline asked. Her voice sounded weary and desperate again.

"Don't worry, Mrs. Kline," Ned told her. "We'll find her. We've got one good lead: We know she's somewhere by the beach." He met Nancy's eyes. They both knew that in Southern California that really didn't mean much.

"I'm calling the police," Mr. Kline said. "They should know about this right away."

"I could use a glass of iced tea," Karen Kline said. "Anyone else?"

"I'll help," Nancy offered, following Mrs. Kline out.

"We should call Mike," Karen Kline said as she took a pitcher down from the cabinet.

"Mike Rasmussen?" Nancy asked, surprised. She took four glasses down from the cupboard and set them on the breakfast bar.

"I like Mike," Mrs. Kline said. "I trust him. Not like this Dennis." She sighed and looked as though she was about to cry again. "I can't help thinking none of this would have happened if Rachel hadn't taken up with him in the first place."

Josh came in through the back door just then. He perked up at the sight of Nancy and Mrs. Kline. "What's going on?"

Mrs. Kline put her arm around her son while Nancy finished making the iced tea. "We heard from Rachel just now. She hung up before we could find out where she was, but we know she's all right."

Josh let out a relieved sigh. "That's great, Mom. She's okay."

"We do know one thing, though," Nancy told him. "I distinctly heard the sound of the ocean in the background. Your sister is somewhere by the water."

Josh looked puzzled for a moment. "That could be anywhere, though. Did it sound like she was calling long distance?" he asked.

Nancy shook her head. On a hunch, she recited the address Lieutenant Heller had given her for Dennis Harper. "Is that near the water?" she asked.

Josh thought for a long moment, then nodded. "Yeah. I think it is."

"It's possible she was calling from there," Nancy said thoughtfully.

"The police checked his place out and didn't see any sign of Rachel. Or Dennis," Josh said.

"True," Nancy agreed. "It may be a long shot, but it's worth a try. Ned and I will go there tomorrow. There's got to be a clue of some kind," she said emphatically. She hoped so, anyway.

Mrs. Kline picked up the tray. "I think you should get Mike to go with you, Nancy," she said as they headed back into the den. "You and Ned shouldn't go alone. I'm going to call him first thing in the morning. I just want this to be over."

"Don't worry, Mrs. Kline," Nancy said reassuringly. "I have a feeling she's okay." Secretly, though, Nancy wondered. What made Rachel Kline hang up so fast? If she really was safe, why couldn't she talk or come home? Nancy knew they'd better find her. And soon.

Everyone was gathered in the dining room for an early breakfast the next morning when Mike Rasmussen showed up. Mr. Kline invited him to join them.

"Thanks," Mike said cheerfully, sitting down. "I've already eaten, but I could use some tea."

Mrs. Morgan poured him a cup from the pot on the side table and set it in front of him.

Mike's face had an eager expression as he looked at Mrs. Kline. "So you heard from

Rachel," he said. "What did she say? Is she okay?"

"She's alive," Mr. Kline replied. "I'm afraid that's about all we know." He touched a napkin to his mouth and set it aside. "We're hoping you can tell us something, Mike. Any little detail we might have overlooked. Are you absolutely sure that Rachel didn't confide in you before she disappeared?"

Mike lowered his eyes for a moment, and his broad shoulders sagged a little. "Rachel stopped talking to me after she gave me back my class ring," he said. He met Mr. Kline's gaze again. "I wish I could help you, I really do, but I don't know any more than you do."

Nancy jumped in. "Ned and I are going to Dennis Harper's place today," she told Mike. "I was hoping you'd come with us. You might notice some sign that Rachel had been there that we'd miss."

"We think Rachel might have been calling from there last night," Josh put in.

"Why?" Mike asked. He hadn't touched his tea.

"We heard the surf in the background," Mr. Kline answered, his face pinched and tired-looking. "I called the police, but Heller was off duty last night," he said with irritation.

"Allen," Mrs. Kline said softly. "They're doing the best they can."

"Well, their best isn't good enough!" snapped Mr. Kline. He was dressed for the office, and he stood and excused himself from the table. "I'll call Lieutenant Heller from my study," he said in quieter tones. Josh left the room with him, since his father was giving him a ride to the studio. Nancy and Ned were going to use Rachel's car.

"Ready?" Nancy asked, turning to Ned.

He nodded, pushing back his chair.

"We'll let you know the second we find anything," Nancy told Karen Kline before they left the dining room. The woman nodded silently, obviously afraid to hope for too much. She had had too many disappointments so far.

Ned, Nancy, and Mike set out for Dennis Harper's apartment a few minutes later, with Mike giving directions.

"Did you and Rachel get along pretty well?" Nancy asked cautiously, turning to look at Mike in the backseat as they sped along the freeway. "Before the breakup, I mean?"

Mike stared out through the side window, and Nancy saw a muscle tighten in his jaw, then relax again. "Most of the time," he answered, without turning his head.

Since Mike seemed to hang out with Jessica so much, Nancy decided to feel him out about the girl. She was especially curious about why Jessica had intimidated Beth in the pizza place the day before. "Are Jessica and Beth good friends?" she asked.

"No way," Mike blurted out. Then, after a long time, he added, "Jessica is nobody's friend."

"Then why does she hang around with your crowd?"

Mike shrugged. "Something to do, I guess."

"What makes her so nasty?" Nancy persisted. "Yesterday she was pretty hard on Beth."

"I don't know," Mike said noncommittally. "I know for a fact that she dislikes Rachel—intensely. That's mainly because she's jealous. Rachel has always been more popular and done better in school." He pointed toward a green and white sign on the edge of the freeway. "Take this exit and turn right," he said.

Ned followed Mike's instructions. "What do you think Beth could know that she's too scared to tell us?" he asked.

"I don't know," Mike said with a shrug of his shoulders.

Nancy shrugged, too, and then concentrated on the road.

Dennis's apartment was in a large, run-down complex within a hundred yards of the beach. After getting out of the car, Nancy checked the mailboxes in the hall and found out that Dennis lived in number seventeen. They found it on the side of the building facing the water, on the ground floor.

Nancy rang the doorbell. "Dennis!" she called out when there was no answer. Nothing came back but the sound of children laughing somewhere nearby and the soothing rush of the waves on the beach. "Try the knob," Ned said.

Nancy reached for it, and it turned. The door of the apartment opened with a little push.

"Dennis?" Nancy called again, stepping slowly over the threshold. The sight of the living room made her draw in her breath sharply. The chairs and sofa were overturned, and the screen on the small TV set had been smashed, scattering shards of glass all over the cheap carpet.

"Be careful," Ned warned, stepping in behind Nancy. "There might still be someone here."

Nancy moved on to the kitchen. All the dishes had been pulled from the cupboards and broken on the floor. Houseplants had been dumped from their pots and ground into the mess of shattered glass, and the cotton curtains had been pulled off the wall, along with the rods that held them.

Mike whistled under his breath. "Somebody is really mad at this guy," he said.

"Or looking for something," Nancy said, remembering the scene in Rachel's room. She went on through the apartment, finding the bedroom and bathroom much the same. There was no sign of either Rachel or Dennis, though.

"Freeze. Police!" ordered a man's voice as Nancy stepped back into the demolished living room.

Lieutenant Heller lowered his gun at the sight of Nancy. "What are you doing here?"

"Looking for Dennis and Rachel," Nancy answered. "The door was open, and we were worried."

The detective returned his revolver to the holster beneath his suit jacket and slowly took in the mess. "I hope you haven't touched anything," he said.

Ned and Mike were standing just behind Nancy, one on either side. "We haven't," Ned said. "We just got here."

"I take it this happened since you were here last time?" Nancy asked, stepping carefully over a broken vase.

The detective nodded. "Yep. My men came by last night. When Mr. Kline let me know Rachel had called, I thought I'd double-check this place. I didn't expect to find it like this, though."

He went to the telephone, lifted the receiver with a handkerchief, and punched in a number with the end of a pen. "This is Heller," he said, then he barked out the address and asked for a fingerprint person.

Mike's gaze landed on a denim jacket lying on the floor. He walked over and picked it up, his face gray. "This is Rachel's," he said, turning around and holding the garment close to his chest for a moment.

"Let me see," Lieutenant Heller said gently.

When Mike held out the jacket, a piece of paper slipped to the floor. Nancy reached for it.

She found her voice shaking as she read the note out loud: " 'We're in terrible trouble. Find us. Please.' "

Chapter
Eleven

As soon as Nancy finished reading the note, Mike leaned back against the wall, clutching Rachel's jacket to him, his eyes fixed on the floor.

Ned looked on with a worried expression on his face. "Do you think Rachel wrote it?" he asked.

"Let me see that," Lieutenant Heller said, holding out his hand.

Mike glanced at the piece of paper as Nancy gave it to the lieutenant. "That's Rachel's handwriting, all right," he said, his voice shaking.

Nancy looked around the ransacked apartment. "What are you going to do now?" she asked the detective.

"Ask for more manpower," the policeman answered. He went back to the telephone and called the station in the same careful way he had before.

Nancy turned to Rachel's ex-boyfriend. "Are you okay, Mike?"

The boy nodded glumly, but his grip on the jacket was still so tight that his knuckles glowed white. "I—I think I just need some fresh air," he said haltingly. He stumbled toward the open door, and Nancy watched as he went down the hall.

"This is hitting him hard," Ned commented to Nancy.

Nancy nodded thoughtfully. "He must still love her," she replied.

The lieutenant completed his phone call and turned back to Nancy and Ned. "Was he all right?" he asked, cocking a thumb toward the door that Mike had taken out. "He looks as though he's been kicked."

"He's the guy who went with Rachel until about a month ago," Nancy explained. "They broke up when Rachel started dating Dennis Harper. Obviously, Mike still cares about her."

"This can't be easy for him," the lieutenant said. Then he went outside to find Mike. Nancy followed, with Ned close behind.

"You seem pretty shook up," the policeman said to Mike, who was sitting on the front steps. "You must care a lot about this girl."

"I do," Mike agreed. Then, quickly, he corrected himself. "Did."

"Mike, is there anything you can think of that would explain why Rachel might be in danger?" Nancy asked.

"Or what might have made her leave that note?" Ned added.

"I know what you think," Mike snapped, still holding Rachel's jacket across his lap. "You think maybe I'm connected with this somehow, that I wanted to get even with Rachel or something! Well, I wouldn't hurt her. I really loved her!"

"That's not what we're saying, son," the lieutenant said in a gentle voice. "We're just looking for some kind of lead."

Mike lowered his head. "I don't know what to tell you. I'm just as confused as you are. All I want is to find her before something really bad happens."

The lieutenant nodded and rose to his feet. "So do we, son. So do we." He paused for a moment. "I'll need the jacket for evidence," he said, holding out one hand. Mike gave the jacket to him.

Two squad cars pulled up, and three uniformed officers—along with the woman who had come to the Klines' to lift fingerprints—came across the narrow lawn.

At the sight of them, Mike got to his feet and stood staring out toward the ocean.

Mike was lost in thought and seemed unaware that Nancy and Ned were standing next to him. "Those cats can be dangerous," he muttered under his breath with a shake of his head.

Nancy touched his arm. "What did you mean just now?" she asked. "About cats being dangerous?"

Mike almost jumped at the question, but he recovered his composure almost immediately. "I just meant 'those guys,' criminals in general," he said. Nancy thought Mike was acting a bit flustered. "Look," he said suddenly, glancing at his watch and trying to smile, "I've got to get to work pretty soon. Think you could drive me back to the Klines' so I can pick up my car?"

"Sure," Ned answered.

"I'll ask the lieutenant if it's okay for us to leave," Nancy added.

Minutes later they were in the Camaro.

Soon after they arrived back at the Klines', Ned and Nancy watched Mike drive off to work.

"Come on, Nickerson," Nancy said, grabbing his hand and leading him back to Rachel's car.

"What's up?" Ned asked.

"I don't know exactly," Nancy said as Ned started up the car. "But I get the feeling Mike's hiding something. Remember what he said about 'those cats'?"

Ned nodded and pulled out into the street. Mike's car was making a turn at a stop sign up ahead.

"I'll bet you anything it's got to do with those cat symbols we've been seeing." She counted them off on her fingers. "Beth's necklace. The graffiti on the wall at the Snake Pit. And this invitation." She pulled it out of her purse.

"So you think Mike knows who these 'Kats' are?" Ned asked.

"There's only one way to find out. I hope if we follow him, we'll learn more."

Up ahead she spied Mike's blue sports car. Ned kept as much distance between the two vehicles as he could without losing sight of Mike.

Soon the sports car zoomed up a freeway

ramp. At the moment, Nancy knew, they were headed in the general direction of Sound Performance, where Mike had said he was going. Still, she recalled what Mike had said about having a few days off. Was he going to work or not?

"I doubt if Mike is involved in Rachel's disappearance, though," Ned threw in as Mike slowed down for an exit. He dropped back a few car lengths, then took the same ramp. "He seemed honestly shook up back there."

"It could have been an act, though," Nancy said. She was almost disappointed when Mike headed straight for Sound Performance, turned into the parking lot beside the store, and got out of his car. She'd been so sure they were on to something.

Ned cruised past to go around the block. "He might know he's being tailed," Ned said. "In which case, he's leading us on a wild-goose chase."

"Or he's really going to work," Nancy said. Ned pulled into the parking lot of the car wash across the street. The sign overhead pictured a big pink elephant, outlined in neon, spraying water out of its trunk. "Maybe. Let's just sit here and watch for a while.

"You know what?" Ned said after a few

minutes. "Why didn't Rachel tell you where she was last night on the phone?"

"There could be an easy explanation," Nancy answered, keeping her eyes on Mike's car. "Maybe she was afraid of being caught talking on the phone."

Just then Mike came strolling out of the front door of Sound Performance. He walked straight toward the parking lot and got into his car.

"Pretty short workday, huh?" Ned said, starting the car.

"I'll say," Nancy agreed.

Mike's sports car made a U-turn, and he drove past them without glancing in their direction. Ned waited a few beats and then pulled out behind him. There were three cars between the Camaro and Mike's sports car.

After driving on the freeway for a while, Mike took an exit leading back to the general vicinity of Dennis's apartment. Nancy sat up a little straighter in her seat, intrigued.

Mike took several unexpected turns, but Ned managed to keep up. Eventually, they were on a street called Beach Drive—the ocean within sight.

The name of the street seemed familiar to Nancy, and she took the Kat Club invitation

out of her purse. Sure enough, the party sched-
uled for that night was being held on Beach
Drive. She had the growing feeling that their
chase had been worthwhile.

A few minutes later Mike stopped in front of
a small two-story beach house. There were cars
parked everywhere, and Nancy and Ned kept
their distance.

"This is it," Nancy whispered, seeing the cat
logo painted above the front door.

"You mean—" Ned began.

Nancy nodded. "Yep. I'll bet you anything
this is the Kat Club."

"That means that for all his denying it at
Dennis's apartment, Mike does know these
Kats! Or is one!"

The words were barely out of Ned's mouth
when Nancy saw two people she knew come
out of the Kat Club and greet Mike—Beth and
Jessica. In her mind she saw Beth playing with
the cat necklace around her neck.

Nancy's words caught in her throat.
"They're Kats, too!"

Chapter

Twelve

"THEY'VE BEEN LYING to us all along!" Nancy said.

Ned grabbed her arm. "Wait a minute. We don't know that they're Kats. We don't have proof that any of them are behind the note we got."

"But they know Kats," Nancy pointed out. "That much is obvious. And they probably know who left that note. Ned, we've got to get in there and find out what's going on."

Ned shook his head. "Not now. There's too much chance of being seen."

"You're right," Nancy agreed reluctantly. "I

guess we'll have to come back tonight as we planned. But, Ned"—Nancy stopped short —"I just had a terrible thought. Suppose they're holding Rachel in there? Her note did say she was in terrible trouble. We know one of the Kats doesn't want us looking for her. What if they're the ones hiding her?"

Ned backed the Camaro around a corner. "Her own friends? Why would they do that?"

Nancy ran a hand through her hair distractedly. "I know it doesn't make sense. Think about it, though—Mike was lying to us about the Kats. He might be lying about not knowing where Rachel is. Beth obviously knows more than she's telling, too."

"It might all be perfectly innocent," Ned pointed out. "Although I doubt it. All I know is, it wouldn't be smart to go in there in broad daylight. Not with so many people around."

Nancy hated leaving when they could be so close to finding Rachel. She knew Ned was right, though. They'd be no help to Rachel if they were caught.

"Next question," Ned said, when they were on the freeway again, headed toward Beverly Hills. "Do we call in the police?"

Nancy considered carefully. "No," she finally answered. "Let's keep this to ourselves until we know what's going on. As you said, we don't have any proof."

"And the Klines?"

"I don't think we should get their hopes up," Nancy said. "We don't even know if she's in there."

Back at the Kline house, the afternoon passed slowly. Mrs. Kline stationed herself by the telephone, hoping for another call from Rachel; Josh and Mr. Kline were both at work.

Nancy felt guilty about not saying anything to her about the Kat Club, but she didn't know what she'd say. They really didn't know who the Kats were or if they were holding Rachel. She still didn't know if Dennis was a Kat, or if he was responsible for Rachel's disappearance. She'd just have to sit and wait until dark and sneak into the Kat Club.

Before dinner that night Nancy changed into black jeans, black sneakers, and a dark sweatshirt. Breaking-and-entering clothes, she thought with a rueful smile, pulling her hair back into a ponytail.

Downstairs she found Ned, who grinned at her and winked.

When Allen Kline came home from work, they all had a quiet dinner beside the pool.

Both the Klines were lost in thought and said very little during the meal.

"Lieutenant Heller told me about Dennis's apartment being ransacked," Mrs. Kline said at one point. "He thinks Rachel might have called us from there. Fingerprints were found that matched some of those in her room. Her jacket was there, too." The woman's composure crumbled, and she began to cry. "And there was that awful note!"

Nancy's thoughts raced. So the person who'd been looking for something in Rachel's room had also tried to find it in Dennis's apartment. But what was that person looking for? Evidence? Proof? Of what? Were the Kats behind the break-ins, too?

After saying good night to the Klines, Nancy and Ned hurried to the nearest freeway entrance. Since there was still a lot of light, they took their time getting to the beach house.

When they got to the Kat Club, the place was all lit up, and even more cars were parked around it than before. Loud music filled the air.

"Okay, Drew, this is it," Ned said, stopping the car well out of sight, around the corner from the Kat Club. "What's the plan?"

"A little romantic stroll along the beach, I think," Nancy said with a smile.

"Then, maybe, we sneak in the back way?"

"You got it."

"Let's agree to stick together as much as possible."

Nancy nodded, and they got out of the car. Circling the club, they made their way around the back to the beach. Nancy could see there was a barbecue on the back deck of the club.

They sneaked up on the beach house, moving through the shadows cast by the other buildings along the shore, and then slipped under the deck. Above them, people were laughing and chattering as loud music continued to blare out. Nancy was grateful for the cover the sound gave them as they knelt down in the sand.

She spotted a basement window and pointed it out to Ned. He nodded, and within a few seconds he had it pried open.

Ned crawled through first, helping Nancy in after him, and they stopped to get their bearings. The place was dark, but after a few moments their eyes adjusted, and they could see a lot of boxes stacked all around them.

Nancy took a penlight from the pocket of her jeans and switched it on. Lifting the lid of one box, she looked inside.

"Ned," she whispered, "there's a VCR in here."

Ned nodded, and they began to check out the other boxes. They found camcorders, stereo components, and more VCRs. Nancy's mind was racing. Why was the basement of the Kat Club full of such valuable items?

Nancy was just about to open her mouth to speak when, at the top of the steps, a door opened, letting in a shaft of light. Ned put a finger to his lips and pulled Nancy behind some boxes. They held their breath as they heard someone move down the stairs and rummage around the basement before heading back upstairs again.

"That was close," Nancy whispered to Ned when they heard the door click closed at the top of the stairs.

"I think the room right up there is full of people," Ned whispered. "Let's look around and see if we can find another way upstairs."

They explored the whole basement, but all they found were more stereos, camcorders, and VCRs.

"Are you wondering what I'm wondering?" Ned asked.

"What's the connection between the Kats and all this equipment?" Nancy whispered back. "You bet I am." She reminded Ned of what Jessica had mentioned about the robberies in Beverly Hills.

"You don't think that was the Kats?" he asked, shaking his head.

"Could be," Nancy said, her excitement rising. "Except if this stuff is stolen, what's it doing in boxes?" she wondered out loud.

"I say we keep exploring a bit more to see what else we can find," Ned said.

"But I think we really have to check out the first floor. We'll have to go up that way eventually," Nancy said, pointing to the stairs.

The door opened just then, and Nancy and Ned barely had time to duck into the shadows again. They stood side by side behind a stack of boxes, their backs to the concrete wall.

"You're getting paranoid, Hanford," came a voice Nancy recognized as Jessica's. "There's nobody down there," she said derisively.

Nancy closed her eyes tightly for a moment and automatically held her breath. After the door closed again, she exhaled.

"I need to hear what they're saying up there," Nancy told Ned.

He squeezed her hand. "Okay. I'm right behind you."

They climbed the stairs with painstaking slowness. Ned feared that someone would open the door to reveal them in a splash of light. They were almost to the top when the knob turned and Jessica's voice said, "Come on, Hanford, we'll go down there right now, and I'll prove to you that you're imagining things."

Ned and Nancy pressed against the wall along the stairs as the door opened a crack and a head peered through.

"I guess you're right," Beth said. "I am being paranoid. But I could have sworn somebody was there when I went down to the freezer to get more steaks for the barbecue."

The door closed again, but not quite all the way. It was open a crack, and Nancy hoped they wouldn't be seen.

Keeping her movements as quiet as she could, Nancy took a quick peek through the opening in the door and saw Beth and Jessica sitting at a kitchen table, drinking sodas. Mike came into the room just then, and Nancy almost gasped out loud when she saw the man behind him.

It was Ralph Lindenbaum, the owner of Sound Performance! What was *he* doing at the Kat Club?

Nancy glanced down at Ned, not daring even to whisper. She put her eye to the keyhole. Jessica was scowling, while Beth looked absolutely terrified. Nancy straightened up and placed her ear against the door to listen to their conversation.

"I'm telling you, Ralph," Mike was saying, "you've got to let me take care of things my way. Nancy Drew and that friend of hers are on to us."

"I'm still running this show, kid," Ralph said furiously. "Besides, Peter Henley's idea is more my style!"

"You promised nobody would get hurt!" Beth cried.

"Oh, shut up," Jessica told her disdainfully. "You're in this as deep as the rest of us, Hanford, and you'd better not get cold feet and blow the whistle on us."

"Nobody is going to turn us in," Ralph insisted.

"Hanford might," Jessica said, her words dripping acid. "She's been acting like a scared rabbit from the first."

Nancy peered through the opening again. Ralph was bending over the girl's chair, his hands on her shaking shoulders, his voice steely. "Don't forget, kid, if we get caught, so do you."

Beth began to sob. "I wish I'd never heard of the Kat Club!" she wailed.

Ned gripped Nancy's sweatshirt and gave a little pull. He didn't need to say anything to let her know they had more than enough information to give the police. It was time to get out.

As he stepped down, though, his step creaked. Desperate to know if the others had heard, Nancy looked directly into the kitchen.

Ralph appeared to be oblivious to the noise, as were Jessica and Mike. Then Nancy glanced at Beth, who was sitting in her direct line of sight.

The girl was staring into Nancy's eyes. Nancy and Ned were caught!

Chapter

Thirteen

NANCY DIDN'T ALLOW HERSELF to panic. As she planned her escape she slowly turned her head from side to side, silently begging Beth not to give her away. For one heart-stopping moment Beth looked uncertain, but then she shifted her gaze.

"What is it now?" Nancy heard Jessica demand sourly.

Beth jumped up and ran out of the room. Nancy let out her breath.

She wanted to stay to check out the rest of the house, but she knew that would be too dangerous. Beth could change her mind at any time and tell Ralph what she'd seen.

Ned caught Nancy by the back of the shirt again and pulled. His message was clear—things were getting too hot, and it was time to leave.

She nodded toward the window where they'd crept in, and then they made their way carefully down the stairs.

Ned gave Nancy a boost up through the window. He was right behind her, and they lay down quietly listening to the party above them on the deck.

Sticking to the shadows, Nancy and Ned fled from the Kat Club as fast as they could.

"We just barely made it out of there," Nancy said breathlessly, once they were both inside the Camaro and Ned was starting up the engine. "Beth looked right at me."

"But she didn't say anything," Ned mused out loud, frowning as he pulled away from the curb.

"No. I think she knows she's in way over her head." Nancy rattled off what they knew. "The Kat Club has to be up to no good. All that stuff in the basement has to be stolen. They know we're on to them, and they're afraid of the police. Ralph Lindenbaum is obviously their ringleader, and maybe Peter Henley."

"So what do we do now?" Ned asked.

"Go back to the Klines' and call Lieutenant Heller," Nancy said with a nod. "He should know about this right away. And so should Rachel's parents."

"But we still don't know where Rachel is, or how deeply involved she and Dennis are," Ned said.

Nancy touched his arm. "Maybe we did find her. She and Dennis might have been at the club. The police can check it out. Let's go."

They made their way through the light freeway traffic back to the Klines'.

"Do you think Rachel could have anything to do with the burglaries in the Hills?" Nancy asked.

"I hope not," Ned answered.

Nancy settled back in her seat and folded her arms. "The Klines probably won't thank us if we find out that Rachel is up to her eyeballs in this whole mess."

"We have to do what's right," Ned reminded her.

Josh was just getting out of a late-model pickup truck as they pulled up. He said a tired goodbye to whoever had given him a lift home and waited in the driveway for Ned to bring the Camaro to a stop.

"I see I'm not the only one who's had a

long day," Josh said. "What have you two been up to?"

Ned sighed. "I think we'd better talk about that inside," he answered. The three of them walked around to the back of the house and entered the kitchen through the rear door.

"I'm starved," Josh confided, opening the refrigerator and peering inside. "We had a dinner break, but that was hours ago. How about you two? Hungry?"

Nancy shook her head. She headed straight for the phone and dialed the police precinct.

"We definitely found the Kat Club tonight," Ned told his friend.

"Please ask Lieutenant Heller to call Nancy Drew at the Kline residence," Nancy said to the officer answering her call, then she hung up. "Ned's getting a little ahead of himself," she said, joining the guys at the breakfast counter. She quickly told Josh about finding Dennis's apartment ransacked and the note Rachel had left.

Ned went on to explain about sneaking into the Kat Club and finding what they assumed was stolen stereo equipment.

Josh sank onto a kitchen stool, his sandwich forgotten. "Do you think Rachel's involved somehow?" he asked quietly.

"We think there's a chance," Nancy said

simply. "They could be holding her some-place. Maybe even there. We really don't know anything about Rachel's part in any of this. I have a call in to Lieutenant Heller."

Josh shoved a hand through his hair. "If they are holding Rachel, they might panic if they see the police coming. They might hurt her."

Nancy had considered that but knew Heller would be careful. "I'm going to talk to Beth Hanford," she said. "Right now. She was really upset at the club, and I think she might have gone straight home. Maybe I can make her see that she's Rachel's only chance—"

Ned touched her shoulder to interrupt her. Nancy looked at Josh. He was staring right through her and appeared to be in shock.

Confused, Nancy gazed up into Ned's grin-ning face. "If you'd stop talking for a minute," he said, "you might stumble over a major clue."

Nancy turned. "What?"

A blond-haired girl was standing in the kitchen doorway. She was tired and rumpled-looking in worn jeans and a flannel shirt. Sobbing, she flung herself into Josh's arms.

Rachel Kline was home.

Chapter

Fourteen

OH, JOSH," RACHEL SAID, gasping through her tears. "I'm sorry—I'm so sorry."

"Take it easy, Rachel," Josh murmured into his sister's hair. "It's okay. You're home now. Everything's going to be okay."

Slowly the girl's sobbing stopped. Her shoulders only moved gently up and down. "Why don't you tell us what happened?" Nancy asked. "It'll make it easier if you talk about it."

Rachel swallowed and shuddered one last time before beginning to talk. "Dennis and I were in hiding at his sister's house," she explained softly. "Last night we went by his apartment to pick up some things he needed. Peter Henley and a couple of the other guys caught us there. I told them I had to go to the bathroom. I wrote a note and put it in my jacket and hoped you'd find it. Then they dragged us to the Kat Club." A haunted look reappeared in Rachel's eyes. "They locked us up in the attic." Her eyes brimmed with fresh tears. "Dennis is still there."

"He's still there? How did you get away?" Nancy asked.

"Jessica untied me so I could use the bathroom," Rachel answered. "There was some kind of scuffle downstairs. When she went to see what it was, I grabbed her from behind. I put my hand over her mouth and pushed her into a closet." She paused, paling as she relived the experience. "She was kicking and yelling, but the music was so loud, nobody could hear her. I put a chair under the knob so she couldn't get out."

Nancy nodded. "And Dennis? Where's he?"

Rachel looked miserable. "Someone was coming up the attic stairs, so I took off. I decided it would be better to go for help than get caught again. I climbed out a window and down a tree." She dried her eyes with the back of one hand. "I'm so afraid of what Peter and the others will do to Dennis when they find out I'm missing."

"I'll call Mom and Dad," Josh said gently. "They've been crazy. We'll get the police to help Dennis."

Rachel reached out and grabbed his arm when he started to walk away. "No. Please. I can't face Mom and Dad until I've done everything I can to make this right, Josh. That's why I left in the first place."

Ned did walk over and dial the police. He left instructions for Heller with the address of the Kat Club.

"Rachel," Nancy began. "Why did you and Dennis take off? What is it you have to make right?" she asked gently.

The girl was silent. She looked uncertainly from Nancy to Ned to Josh. "I can't explain," she said finally. "We have to get back there as soon as possible."

"First I'm letting Mom and Dad know you're back," Josh said firmly. "And where we're going." He headed for the door.

"No! Please, Josh!" Rachel started to cry again.

Nancy stepped in. "Hold it a second, Josh." She turned to the girl. "Rachel," she said gently, "why are you so afraid to tell them you're back?"

"Because then I'll have to explain why I left. And I can't do that until I make everything right," she repeated.

"Why did you leave?" Nancy prodded.

"And why on graduation day?" Ned asked. "Was something going to happen?"

Ned's question set the wheels turning in Nancy's mind. "Were the Kats about to frame you and Dennis?" she asked.

The look of surprise and fear that passed over Rachel's face told Nancy she was right. "Tell us about it," she prodded.

"Beth told me Peter was going to plant stolen equipment in Dennis's car," Rachel explained in a rush. "Stuff from Sound Performance. Ralph had already fired him to set it up."

"Why would Peter do that?" Nancy asked.

Rachel bit down hard on her lower lip. "I think he knew Dennis and I were . . ." The girl's voice started shaking, and she had a hard time going on. Rachel's predicament was obviously tearing her apart.

"Did Peter think you were going to rat on the Kats?" Ned asked.

"About what?" Josh asked. "I'm still confused about what's going on here," he said, raking a hand through his hair in frustration.

Nancy explained, going on her hunches and what the girl had said so far. "Rachel and Dennis were going to tell the police that the Kats were behind the robberies in Beverly Hills. They knew because they had taken part in them. Am I right?" she asked Rachel.

The girl lay down her head on the breakfast counter. A slow nod was her only answer.

Josh was obviously shocked. Instinctively, he reached over to stroke his sister's hair. "It's okay, Rach. Don't cry. It'll be okay."

"Rachel," Nancy began, "I know this isn't easy, but you've got to tell us everything. How did you get involved in the first place?"

Josh continued, "Nancy's right. You made a big mistake, but you've got to tell us the whole story."

"I can't," Rachel moaned softly.

"It's the only way out," Ned said. "Tell us who put you up to it. Was it Ralph?"

Rachel's head shot up. "Ralph! How do you know about Ralph?"

"You just said he fired Dennis to help set up Peter's frame," Nancy pointed out. "We saw him tonight at the Kat Club. Just how is he involved?" she asked.

Rachel paused for a moment and looked at

the three of them. "He sold the stuff we took," she admitted finally.

It all made sense. Ralph fenced stolen equipment from his store, selling it as new. He must have erased the serial numbers, replaced them with phony ones, and used his connections to get empty boxes to put the equipment in. His customers never knew they were getting used equipment. The warranties were probably forged, too. "And it was his idea for you to steal it in the first place?" Nancy asked.

"We didn't have any choice," Rachel said in a whisper.

"I don't understand," her brother said, confused.

Rachel's words echoed in Nancy's ears. They didn't have any choice. "Did Ralph have something on you?" she asked on a hunch.

"Yes, he did," Rachel admitted quietly.

"What was it?" Ned asked, sensing they were about to get to the bottom of Rachel's trouble.

"I guess I'll have to show you," she said in a resigned voice. "You know everything else."

With that, she led the way out of the kitchen and into the den, where Nancy and Ned had watched a movie. She went to the shelf of neatly filed movies and ran her finger over the backs of the cases until she found what she wanted. Rachel pulled out the *Casablanca* tape. When Nancy had tried to play it, she had thought it was blank.

Rachel put the tape into the VCR and turned on the machine and the TV. There was nothing but snow on the screen until Rachel pressed Fast Forward, stopping about halfway through the tape. She pressed Stop and Play, and a shadowy scene took shape.

Nancy watched closely, unable at first to figure out what was going on.

Then she recognized the inside of Sound Performance, the stereo equipment store. There were five shadowy figures moving around, picking up different items and carefully carrying them to the back of the store.

Nancy took a step closer to the screen. One by one, Nancy identified the people—Jessica, Beth, Mike, Peter, Rachel, and another, whom she assumed to be Dennis.

She realized that what they were watching was the store security tape—showing the members of the Kat Club stealing from Sound Performance!

Chapter

Fifteen

WHEN THE TAPE went blank again, Josh reached out and punched off the VCR. Nancy could tell that Ned's friend was in shock. Rachel covered her face with both hands. "I—I don't know what to say, Josh," she whispered. "I never meant for any of this to happen."

Nancy put a hand on Rachel's shoulder. "What exactly did happen? Why did you rob the store?"

Rachel gazed at Nancy with miserable, red-rimmed eyes. "I didn't want to do this, and neither did Beth. But the guys—Mike and Peter—kept pressuring us. They said it was a practical joke they wanted to play on Ralph—Mr. Lindenbaum."

"You didn't think you'd be caught?" Ned asked in a surprised voice.

"Beth and I figured nobody would get in trouble if it was only a joke. Besides, the guys told us that since we knew about it, we were already involved." She paused and tossed her long hair back over one shoulder. "I know it was stupid, but we went along," she added, her voice shaking.

"Tell us about the rest of it in the car on the way back to the club," Nancy gently suggested.

"We carried the things outside to a truck parked in back," Rachel continued in the back seat. "Mike said we were going to give everything back after Mr. Lindenbaum stewed for a bit. Since he worked there, I guess he suspected Ralph was already selling stolen stuff. He didn't think Ralph would have the guts to report our robbery to the police. We didn't take much—only enough to worry him."

"What made Mike want to do it in the first place?" Josh asked.

"He's into dares," Rachel explained. "At least he was, before this. When Peter suggested it to him, they thought it would be kind of fun. Shake Ralph up a bit."

"That didn't happen, though, did it?" Nancy asked, turning to look at Josh and Rachel.

Rachel choked back her tears. Josh reached out and drew his sister to him for the first time since he'd seen the tape. "Go on, Rachel," he said calmly.

"No, it didn't," Rachel said, with her brother's arm securely wrapped around her. "Ralph called each of us and told us we'd better be at his store that night at closing time or we'd end up in jail."

"So you went?" Ned prompted gently.

Rachel nodded. "We were scared not to. When we got there, we found out we were in big trouble."

"So he put you up to robbing houses?" Josh asked, his anger evident.

"He showed us the tape," Rachel explained. "We hadn't thought about it."

"How did you get the tape?" Ned wanted to know.

"Dennis stole it the night before we went into hiding," Rachel explained.

"So Ralph used the tape to blackmail you into burglarizing houses," Nancy concluded.

Rachel nodded again glumly. "Yes."

"You were perfect for the job: You all came from this area, except for Dennis, so you knew which houses had alarms and how to beat some of them," Nancy went on.

"Why would this Lindenbaum character want a bunch of kids to steal for him?" Josh demanded.

"He knew how to doctor the serial numbers," Nancy explained, "so he could sell any stolen stuff in his store. Since he had something on them, the Kats were useful to him. Am I right?" she asked Rachel.

"Yes," the girl confessed quietly.

"That still doesn't explain why you ran away," Josh said to his sister.

"I think she wanted to get out of the ring, Josh," Ned said from the driver's seat. "Along with Dennis."

"When Beth told me Dennis was going to be framed," Rachel explained, "we got scared. We decided to run away until we had proof against Ralph and Peter."

"Why didn't you just come to us?" Josh asked. "Mom and Dad would have helped."

"Sometimes people don't think rationally when they're scared," Nancy said, glancing at the clock on the dashboard. "Speed it up just a bit, Ned. We should get to Dennis quickly."

Rachel's eyes took on a haunted look. "I

don't know if they'll hurt him. When they found us, they couldn't decide what to do with us. But now when they find out I'm gone . . ."

"I hope Lieutenant Heller is there already," Nancy said. "You did tell him to meet us, Ned, didn't you?"

Ned nodded. "I didn't talk directly to him. I only left a message," he added.

"What about all those other kids who were at the party tonight?" Nancy asked Rachel. "Were they blackmailed into stealing, too?"

Rachel swallowed hard. "Some of them were into it—like Jessica. They thought it was a kick. You know how it is." At that, she lowered her eyes for a moment, finding it difficult to face Nancy. "My mom and dad are just going to die when they find out what I did."

Nancy reached out and took Rachel's hand for a moment. She told her about how her room had been broken into. "Do you think one of them was looking for the tape that showed you robbing the store?" she asked.

After a long time Rachel nodded. "Probably. It could have been Peter. He turned Dennis's apartment upside down trying to find it while we were there. We told him Dennis didn't have it."

"He must have known you needed it to take

to the police," Ned pointed out. "To prove that Ralph was blackmailing you."

"I guess," Rachel said, nodding.

Ned took the Beach Drive exit and brought the car to a stop in the same place where he and Nancy had parked earlier. All but three cars were gone from the front of the club. The music had been turned off, but lights were still on inside the beach house.

Rachel scanned the cars. "Mike and Ralph and Peter are still here," she said.

"We'll have to be really careful," Nancy said. "By now they must know you're gone. They'll be looking for us. I wonder where Lieutenant Heller is. Why wouldn't the police be here by now?"

After a short conference the four decided the basement window would be the best way to get in. Ned crawled through first, then Nancy, then Josh, and finally Rachel.

"Come on," Nancy said, heading toward the stairs. Ned was right behind her, with Rachel close behind him.

Josh stopped Rachel. "Let Nancy and Ned go first," he said in a low voice. "They've had experience at this stuff."

Reluctantly Rachel agreed. Nancy started up the steps, her heart pounding. There was a chance their break-in could fail. If they were caught, it would be a matter of stalling for time until the police showed up. Where were they? she wondered again.

The kitchen light was out, and the door squeaked a little as Nancy pushed it open.

She waited to see if anyone had heard the sound. When no one came, she pushed the door a little farther. It glided open, nearly crashing against the wall. Moving silently, Nancy crept into the kitchen and looked both ways.

There was a pantry on the right, but it was empty. To the left was a lighted hallway.

When Ned, Josh, and Rachel had all joined her in the kitchen, she turned to face them. "We'll search the first floor," she whispered. "Everybody, be careful!"

The first room off the kitchen was cluttered and had a view of the ocean. There was a computer set up on a desk in front of the window. Nancy stole closer and saw a pile of disks. One was clearly labeled Inventory.

Very efficient, she thought. Ralph Lindenbaum was keeping a record of all stolen merchandise.

Nancy picked up the small plastic disk and tucked it into the pocket of her jeans. Lieutenant Heller would find it fascinating reading.

Another room opened off that one, and two

more after that. The entire floor appeared to be empty.

Reaching the foot of the stairs leading to the second floor, Nancy braced herself. Quietly she stole up the stairs, stopping when she heard voices behind a door at the far end of the dark hallway. A slice of golden light shone out from under the door. Just to her left were stairs that Nancy knew must lead to the attic.

Signaling the others to remain hidden, Nancy sneaked forward until she had reached the door with the light shining around its edges. Drawing a deep breath and letting it out slowly, Nancy crouched and peered through the keyhole. She couldn't see much, just the back of someone's T-shirt.

"I say we get rid of him tonight," she heard Peter saying. "Rachel got away, and she's probably spilled the whole thing by now. I don't know about you two, but I'm taking my share of the money and getting out of here!"

Nancy's heart hammered against her rib cage as she heard footsteps in the room moving toward her. At the last second they stopped.

"I'm going to Mexico," Mike said dismally. "There are probably warrants out for our arrest right now."

"Don't be so sure she's talked," said Ralph.

"She knows we've still got Dennis. I bet she hasn't said a word. She really cares about that guy."

"Don't remind me," Mike snapped.

"If she doesn't talk," Peter put in, "Beth will. She's been on the verge of breaking for days."

Nancy got up from her crouched position and eased backward along the hallway, keeping her eye on the door the whole time.

Just then, the door opened.

Nancy darted up onto the attic steps. Rachel was already there. They could only guess where Ned and Josh were. It was too dark to see, and they didn't dare move.

"I'm not going to stick around here waiting for the cops to show up," Peter said.

Nancy prayed they wouldn't decide to check on Dennis right then. If they did, they'd run right into her and Rachel. Rachel's rapid breathing sounded so loud to Nancy that she was sure it would give them away. She just hoped the three men wouldn't hear it. They were standing so close that Nancy could have reached out and touched them.

Ralph was shaking his finger in Peter's face. One glance to the left, and he'd be looking straight at them. "The trouble with you, kid," he lectured, "is that you're too hotheaded. You act first and think later. That leads to mistakes."

Nancy's heart was beating so hard she thought it was going to burst at any moment. She ran her tongue over her lips and waited. Where were Ned and Josh?

"Like pushing Nancy Drew off the deck at the Beckers' party," Mike said with contempt. "And trying to run her and her boyfriend down with a car!"

"Shut up, Rasmussen," Peter warned.

So it was Peter who had tried to scare her off that night at the party. And Peter who had nearly run her and Ned over!

Lindenbaum slapped both boys on the back and said, "Now, now, no arguing. Let's go downstairs and figure out a good, solid plan. We're okay as long as we don't lose our heads."

If Ned and Josh had hidden on the stairs, they were about to get caught. Nancy held her breath. Luckily Ralph and the boys went past them and down the stairs without incident.

"Ned!" Nancy whispered into the darkness, afraid to use her flashlight. "Where are you?"

A nearby door opened soundlessly, and Ned and Josh appeared. Rachel didn't waste any time in leading the way up the attic steps. Pushing the door at the top open, the girl ran into the lighted attic.

Dennis, a good-looking guy with spiky brown hair and wearing jeans and a white T-shirt, was sitting in a chair, his hands and feet tied. When he saw them, his eyes lit up.

Nancy immediately began untying him while Rachel bent to put her arms around his neck. "You didn't think I wouldn't come back, did you?" she said.

"You should have stayed away," Dennis replied, a worried tone in his voice. "You know how dangerous those guys are."

"I couldn't leave you here," Rachel insisted.

Nancy finished untying Dennis's ankles. She looked over to where Ned was keeping watch at the top of the attic steps. There wasn't any time to waste. They had to get out fast.

"Who are these people?" Dennis asked, standing and trying to get the circulation going in his legs.

"It's okay," Rachel said, reassuring him. "This is my brother Josh, and his friend Ned Nickerson is over there. This is Nancy Drew."

Dennis nodded slowly. "You told them, didn't you?" he whispered to Rachel.

"I had to," she answered. "It's all over, Dennis."

"We have to get out of here fast," Nancy said firmly. "Can you make it out that window and down the tree?" she asked Dennis.

He shook his head, indicating his legs were still too shaky.

Nancy grabbed Ned's hand and led the way carefully back downstairs. She kept her eyes wide open for any sign of Mike, Peter, or Ralph.

They made it safely down to the first floor. Nancy could barely hear Ralph's booming voice. It sounded as though it was coming from the deck outside. With a wave of relief she realized that if they were really careful, they could head back out through the basement.

Nancy led the way into the kitchen, Rachel and Dennis right behind her, Josh and Ned bringing up the rear.

Just as she was opening the door to the basement Nancy heard a voice behind her.

"Welcome to the Kat Club."

She turned to see Ralph, Peter, and Mike standing in the doorway leading to the deck. Ralph's hands held a drawn gun as he smiled at his uninvited guests.

She looked over at her friends' shocked faces. They were caught.

Chapter

Sixteen

THESE TWO," Ralph went on, smiling sardonically at Dennis and Rachel, "aren't going anywhere. They know too much." His gaze took in Nancy, Ned, and Josh. "Now, of course, you do, too."

Nancy swallowed. Whatever happened, she couldn't lose her cool. "It's too late, Mr. Lindenbaum. You can't get away with this."

Ralph ignored her. His smile had faded, and he was glaring at Dennis. "You know, you should have been in jail already."

"Why?" Nancy put in. "Because you tried to

frame him for stealing equipment from your store?"

Ralph gave Nancy a shocked look. "We're on to you," Ned told him. "We know what you've been up to."

Dennis put his arm around Rachel, but his eyes never left Ralph's gun. "You're a creep, you know that, Lindenbaum," he sneered. "And that frame was the lowest. I knew you'd guessed that Rachel was about to break down and tell her folks what was going on, so you decided to pin the blame for everything on me."

Nancy glanced at Rachel, then at Ned and Josh. She made a sign that told him he should be prepared to jump Ralph and Dennis and Peter. Ned gave her an almost imperceptible nod.

"I want the security tape, Rachel," Ralph said. "The one that shows you kids robbing Sound Performance."

Rachel shook her head. "It's over, Ralph," she said steadily. "Give up."

Lindenbaum held his gun steady on Rachel. "The other Kats are willing to pretend the whole thing never happened!" he said furiously. "Why couldn't you cooperate?"

He reached out and grabbed Rachel by the arm, shoving the gun into her rib cage. "Now

I'll tell you what you're going to do, little lady," he crooned into her ear. "You're going to tell me where that tape is, and do you know why? Because your boyfriend Dennis and all your friends here are going to be in real danger until I give the word to let them go, that's why!"

"Let her go," Dennis said, his eyes flashing.

Ralph laughed. "Let's take them upstairs and tie them up," he said as Peter drew a gun of his own and held it on them.

"Let's go!" Peter barked, his eyes glinting. "Everybody up to the attic!"

"Anybody tries anything," Ralph warned, "and the girl gets shot."

There was nothing to do but put their hands up and do as Ralph said. Even if Ned and Nancy could have gotten the jump on Peter, Ralph was still holding his gun on Rachel at very close range.

As they climbed the attic stairs, though, Nancy was already devising a plan. They'd have to act fast, before their hands and feet were tied.

"Wait a minute!" Mike rasped, hovering in the doorway once they were all in the attic. "I'm not going along with anything like this! Let Rachel go, Ralph. You're hurting her!"

Peter turned on him. "As if you cared. Get

the rope, Rasmussen!" he snarled. "And I'm not going to tell you twice!"

In that moment Nancy's eyes met Mike's. She asked him a silent question: Who will it be, Mike—them or us?

She drew a deep breath and signaled to Ned. Her eyes turned toward Peter. She silently counted to three, then threw herself at Peter's knees.

The boy's gun flew out of his hand and fell to the floor, out of reach. With Ned's help Nancy wrestled him to the floor.

Rachel began screaming at the top of her lungs. The result was ear-shattering. Then she stomped down hard on Ralph's instep, and he howled in pain and rage and dropped his gun. Nancy scooped it up in one quick motion.

Josh caught Mike by the back of the collar before he could escape down the stairs. He threw him roughly to the attic floor.

Mike just sat there with his hands away from his sides to show he didn't want any part of the fight.

Dennis went to Rachel and took her in his arms. The girl burst into tears. "It's over," she murmured into his shoulder. "I can't believe it's finally over."

Nancy and Ned tied Ralph and Peter to the poles that supported the attic ceiling while

Josh pushed a scowling Mike into the chair where Dennis had been held and bound his hands behind his back.

"Come on, Ned," she said, "let's go downstairs and wait for the police."

Rachel was drying her eyes. "Come on, Dennis," she said sadly. "Let's go with them. I don't want to be in the same room with these guys."

"You'll never prove anything!" Ralph spat out, glaring at Nancy.

"Oh, no?" she asked. "This basement is full of stolen goods. I bet the lease on this place is in your name. We've also got a roomful of people who are willing to testify that you blackmailed them into stealing for you." She paused, pulled the computer disk from her pocket, and held it up. "Your inventory. This should be proof enough, I think."

"I'll keep an eye on them while you go downstairs and wait for the police," Josh said to Nancy and Ned. "Look out for Rachel, will you? She's pretty upset."

Ned slapped his friend on the back. "Don't worry, buddy. Everything's okay now."

Downstairs Rachel was sitting at the kitchen table with Dennis. She looked up as Nancy sat down at the table next to her. "What's going to happen to us?" she asked.

"I'm not sure," Nancy replied. "Burglary is a felony, but the judge might be lenient because Ralph coerced you."

"My mom and dad are going to be so upset!"

"I'm sure they'll deal with it. The most important thing to them is your safety."

"What about Peter?" Rachel asked. "And Mike?"

Nancy sighed. "My guess is that the courts will be pretty hard on Peter, considering what he did."

"His parents are going to be really angry," Rachel said.

"I honestly don't know about Mike, but he's obviously in pretty deep," Nancy said.

Rachel nodded sadly. "Where's Josh?"

"Upstairs, standing guard," Ned replied, laying a hand on Rachel's shoulder.

At that moment three uniformed officers came into the kitchen, their guns drawn. Lieutenant Heller was close behind.

He looked as if he'd dressed hurriedly, and he was surprised when he saw Nancy. "Sorry for the delay. They didn't call me right away. They thought Ned's call was a prank. Someone who knew about the case saw the note, and then we got into high gear. So tell me what's happening."

"We got Rachel back and solved the Beverly

Hills robberies. The ringleader is Ralph Lindenbaum—he's upstairs, in the attic, with his right-hand man, Peter Henley, and Mike Rasmussen," Nancy replied.

The lieutenant's gaze fell on Rachel. "Hello there, young lady," he said kindly. "We've been looking for you."

"Rachel and Dennis have a few things they want to tell you," Nancy said quietly.

The detective got out his notebook and sat down at the table. The uniformed officers, in the meantime, were going up to bring down Ralph, Mike, and Peter.

"Read them their rights, then take them downtown and book them," Heller said without looking away from Rachel and Dennis. "Now let's hear it, kids—right from the start."

Slowly, haltingly at first, Rachel explained how she and Beth and Jessica had joined in the robbery at Sound Performance, thinking it was a practical joke. Then she went on to say that Ralph had used the security tape, which had been running that night, to blackmail them into committing further burglaries.

"What about you, Dennis?" the lieutenant asked quietly when Rachel had finished speaking. "How did you get involved?"

Dennis lowered his eyes for a moment, then met the lieutenant's gaze squarely. "I'm guilty," he said. "I guess I pretty much knew what was going on when Rasmussen and Henley planned the rip-off at Sound Performance. I should have stopped them from getting the girls to join in, but I didn't."

"I'm going to have to take you and Rachel down to the station for questioning," the detective said. "And I have to be honest with you—there's every chance that you'll be charged, Dennis."

Dennis swallowed visibly, and his arm tightened around Rachel's shoulders. "What about Rachel?"

"I don't know. One thing I do know, though—I need the names of all the other kids who were involved."

Rachel lifted her eyes to Josh's face, and her brother nodded solemnly. "Beth Hanford," she began in a small, shaky voice. "Jessica Bates . . ."

It was late when Mr. Kline brought an ashen-faced Rachel home from the police station. His face was grim as he greeted his anxious wife. "Charges have been filed against all the kids," he said. When Mrs. Kline gasped, he added, "Our attorney thinks Rachel will probably get a long probationary period and some public service, since she was essentially coerced into the crime. Dennis may get off lightly, too, since he was prepared to go to the police when he and Rachel took off."

"What about Ralph and Peter?" Nancy asked.

"Lindenbaum is being charged with grand theft, kidnapping, and conspiracy," Mr. Kline explained. "Henley, too, only he's got assault and attempted murder added on for good measure."

Mrs. Kline put her arms around Rachel. "You're exhausted, dear. You have to get some sleep. And so should you," she said, turning to her son.

Josh shook his head. "I'm due at the studio in an hour," he said. "I'll just take a shower and grab some breakfast."

Nancy was exhausted, but she knew she was probably too wound up to sleep. "What about Jessica and Mike?" she asked. "What's going to happen to them?"

Rachel looked sad. "They'll probably have to go to jail for a while."

"And Beth?"

"She wanted to tell from the first," Rachel said. "And you said she didn't give you away when she saw you peeking out of the cellar door."

"There's one last thing," Nancy said, remembering how Dennis had disappeared from the Snake Pit that night. "What was Dennis doing at the club if you two were laying low?"

"He wanted to reason with Peter," Rachel said. "I told him it was useless, but he wouldn't listen to me. Then, when he saw Mike and everyone else there, he was afraid he'd be caught. That's why he took off."

"What I don't understand is why you let this go on so long," Karen Kline said to her daughter in a sad voice. "Why didn't you call us sooner? You knew we'd have helped."

Rachel sighed. Nancy could tell it was the one thing the girl couldn't really explain. "I thought Dennis and I could take care of it ourselves. We'd gotten into the mess, and somehow we had to get out of it."

"Don't ever think that way again," Allen Kline told his daughter. "You know we're here for you, no matter what you do."

"It wasn't easy for you, was it, Rachel?" Nancy asked, genuinely concerned.

The girl swallowed hard and looked at her family. "No. I'm just glad it's all over."

"Me, too," Josh said, and he turned to Ned and Nancy. "Now maybe you two can have that vacation you planned."

Karen Kline smiled at her son's effort to

cheer them all up. Allen put an arm around his daughter.

Nancy hooked her arm through Ned's. "That sounds great. I have to admit I'm ready for a little relaxation."

Ned grinned at her. "Me, too. For a while there it was beginning to look like we'd have to go back to River Heights to get it!"

"What would you say to a nice romantic walk on the beach?" Nancy suggested playfully.

"No spying on anyone?" Ned asked with a gleam in his eye.

"No spying," Nancy assured him. "This time it'll be the real thing."

Nancy's next case:

Summer in the Hamptons—a posh New York beach resort—promises plenty of fun in the sun. What more could Nancy and her friends want? Maybe a touch of romance and a dash of mystery. An international dance workshop is in town, and Nancy's aunt Eloise is sponsoring Soviet dancer Sasha Petrov. But Sasha plans on sponsoring Nancy—as a partner in love.

Then allegations of espionage swirl around the dancers. George's new boyfriend, test pilot Gary Powell, is in the middle of it when his company accuses him of stealing a top-secret blueprint. Nancy is determined to clear Gary's name, but she fears making a wrong move with Sasha; perhaps he's a master of deceit as well as a master of the dance . . . in *A DATE WITH DE-CEPTION*, Case #48 in the Nancy Drew Files™ and the first book in the Summer of Love trilogy.